Mechcraft
DISRUPTION

Brian Fitzpatrick

Black Rose Writing | Texas

ISBN: 978-1-68433-680-7
PUBLISHED BY BLACK ROSE WRITING
www.blackrosewriting.com

Printed in the United States of America
Suggested Retail Price (SRP) $17.95

Mechcraft: Disruption is printed in Garamond Premier

*As a planet-friendly publisher, Black Rose Writing does its best to eliminate unnecessary waste to reduce paper usage and energy costs, while never compromising the reading experience. As a result, the final word count vs. page count may not meet common expectations.

For Luke and Jonathan. Our friendship, collaborations, reviews, and notes have pushed my creativity to levels I never could have achieved on my own. Your sound advice has benefitted me at every turn. Thank you for our amazing meetups; looking forward to more.

Special thanks to editor extraordinaire, Sheila Shedd, for making my words soar, while keeping me grounded.

Thanks go out as well to my ever-supportive wife, Teresa, my creative son, Tyler, and my eternally encouraging parents and extended family. You have all been my rock.

Lastly, to Black Rose Writing for adding me to their roster of talented authors. Thank you for this incredible opportunity.

Mechcraft
DISRUPTION

CHAPTER 1

Downtown Los Angeles existed behind the allure and broken dreams of Hollywood and in the background of coveted beaches famous the world over. With all the allure of the region, downtown went largely ignored by the visiting masses, just a regrettably plain guest at an otherwise glamorous party. Locals emerged in the modernized streets for shopping, or a play at the Ahmanson, a concert at the Walt Disney Hall, or, more often, an unfortunate courthouse visit. But tourists rarely ventured there.

The January sky cast a grey haze over the landscape, leaving most yearning for the sun that typically bathed the city in warm, golden light.

Hiding in plain sight stood a nondescript, nine-story, black glass building. To the casual passerby, the structure left no imprint, an instantly forgotten aspect in a city brimming with false fronts. But behind the veneer of normalcy, inside the monolithic structure, a community of gifted people existed who worked behind the scenes to manipulate the path of humankind.

The deserted street passing the front of the building lay clean and unbloodied. All evidence of the countless bodies that had strewn the pavement from that horrible, prophetic night three months ago had been completely erased. The damage to nearby buildings, ruined landscaping, gouges in the asphalt had all been repaired by specialists from within the building. Even the ghosts of the many dead seemed to have moved on;

three months was a long time, but some scars took longer to heal than streets and structures.

Jake London, a slender, unassuming fifteen-year-old, shook away thoughts of metal and blood, and focused on his task. He strode the halls of the Phalanx headquarters, heading toward the prison cells. He passed through corridors lined with metallic tendrils that glowed with vivid colors, pulsing with life of their own. He smiled at his peers as they passed, making their way swiftly to classes or training. Most returned the smile, but some still steered clear of him, frightened.

He entered the open courtyard and marveled at the display of moving, writhing, liquid metal. He looked up; the show continued on, several stories above him. At the ground level, students casually conjured liquid nanotech from their palms and telepathically manipulated the material into shapes of wonder and curiosity.

Mechcraft was a godlike power, and Jake sometimes still feared the nanotechnology that coursed through his veins. And no matter how long he stayed in the Phalanx headquarters, he would never be able to relate to his peers for one simple difference: he was the only person on earth born with the nanotech already infused into his DNA. Every other Mechcrafter had to undergo a voluntary process of rigorous screening, a series of excruciating injections and, then, years of training to evolve the coveted ability. It didn't come easy. All the students around him had asked for this, sacrificed for it. He couldn't wrap his mind around that concept. *Who would choose this terrifying power?*

No time for philosophical musings.

Jake had been summoned to the prison, and he knew exactly why. He'd been dreading this inevitable confrontation. His stomach churned and his legs felt numb as he walked on. He revealed this to no one, but nightmares still plagued his dreams. Sasha was still in his head. The maniacal leader of the Hunter faction had pursued him relentlessly, kidnapped and tortured him, attempted to brainwash him, tried to force him to murder innocent people. Finally, in the streets in front of the Phalanx building, she had waged all-out war against him and his family. And now Dr. Flint wanted him to have a chat with her.

He took some solace that the Hunter faction had crumbled that night, but that did not alleviate his trepidation at having to face Sasha again after all these months. Jake reached the guarded doorway of the prison area. Two stiffs in black suits scrutinized the lanky, scruffy-haired teen before them, and with some caution and much authority, waved him through. He checked in at the registrar's desk, and a barred door turned to liquid and parted, allowing him passage.

Walking the hall, he was actually happy to see more and more empty cells. After their capture, the Hunter faction members had initially resisted attempts by Phalanx to assimilate them and redirect their mindset away from the violence that had been drilled into them. Sasha's brainwashing had proved far more thorough than anyone expected. The Hunter agents, mostly teens, would rather fight than listen to reason. The factor that ultimately cracked their armor was Jake and his terrifying power. During the Disruption Day battle—as it became known—Jake completely obliterated every mech weapon the Hunters conjured, rendering them all powerless.

They were then forced to witness Jake's punishment of their leader...words could not describe the blasphemous act. Telepathically seizing control of Sasha's nanos, Jake forced them back into her body, nearly killing her. Intimidation had kept their prisoners in line at first, but, eventually, through patience and communication, the Phalanx deprogrammers began to see success in bringing Hunters out of their religious fervor and worship of Sasha.

More and more Hunters denounced the cultists they had once been, and, after proving their trustworthiness, were permitted to become productive members of Phalanx. The dozen cells that lined the path were now more than half empty.

Those still resistant to change saw Jake approaching and scrambled to the backs of their cells. He ignored them as best he could; their anxiety stirred in him a guilt he knew he should not feel. Yet it still crept up whenever a fellow Mechcrafter showed fear of him.

He neared the end of the cells and froze. To his left, one boy stood at the cell door, unafraid of him. He looked over to see his former best friend,

Scott. He couldn't miss that red hair. Both teens stood motionless, not knowing what to say. Scott's betrayal hung heavy in the air. It was he who had brought Sasha and the Hunter agents to Jake's door in the first place, setting in motion the terrible events of the following days. Because of Scott's false loyalty, many people had died. Jake thought he saw the weight of that knowledge in his eyes, but perhaps that was only a reflection of his own sadness. Jake wanted to speak, but the words would not come. He only sighed and started walking again.

"I'm sorry," Scott muttered weakly.

Jake paused, almost turned around, but kept going. Scott's shoulders sank and he sat down in tortured silence.

*   *   *

Dr. Max Flint met Jake at the door to the control room. He no longer needed his trademark cane, and his wrinkled skin had taken on a more youthful shine. The ending of a two-decade war had done wonders for the soul. Dr. Flint had led Phalanx through all the years of violence and animosity, the long war between the factions, and had proven up to the challenge.

"Thank you for coming, Jake," he began in an unusually jovial tone. "We appreciate this more than you know, dear boy."

"Happy to help," he lied. He could already feel the nervous sweat beading on his forehead. He swept his brown hair away from his eyes. His face burned, and he found himself scratching at the fine hair that had begun to invade his jawline the past couple months.

In the control room, four agents sat at computer-laden desks and, through a large glass window, observed a woman in a separate, isolated cell constructed of thick, clear Plexiglas.

Jake could see her from the corner of his eye, but he could not bring himself to look directly at her. Dr. Flint escorted him deeper into the chamber; still he could not look to his left. They stopped at an agent who sat in front of a microphone.

"Any progress, Ben?" asked Dr. Flint.

Agent Ben Donovan let out an exasperated sigh. "Same shit."

Remembering his manners, Dr. Flint motioned, "Jake, this is Ben Donovan, Head of Security. Ben, this is—"

"I know who he is," Ben interrupted, unimpressed. He looked up to meet Jake's eyes. Ben wore frustration across his face. He looked exhausted; his eyes darkly ringed, his normally well-styled hair and goatee two weeks overgrown and speckled with more gray than they should be. "You certainly are the man of the hour. Thanks for coming."

Staring at the frail female in the cell, her black hair a tangled mess hanging over her face, Dr. Flint seemed to ponder a decision.

He turned to Ben. "Try one more time."

"She's a broken record, but alright."

Ben leaned into the mic. "Sasha, you need to tell us. It's the only way to keep your people safe."

He was met with silence.

Dr. Flint noticed Jake's eyes cast downward. "Jake, its fine. She can't see us in here. You can face her."

Slowly Jake lifted his gaze toward the cell in the other room. What he saw disturbed him more than if Sasha had been in all her fearsome glory. In the cell sat the husk of a woman, pale and fragile. Her hair, once a raven mane, cascaded in jagged black tangles down her front, and obscured most of her face. She heaved repeatedly, trying half-heartedly to mask the sobs that shook her body. She wore loose cotton pants and a baggy shirt, psyche hospital garb 101. She'd tossed her flip flops into a corner, choosing the cold floor for her bare feet.

Patience worn thin, Ben prodded, "Sasha, we can do this for the rest of your life."

Sasha only rocked back and forth, then frantically scratched at her left arm.

Ben turned off the mic, and looked up at Dr. Flint. "It ain't happening. I still say we force it out of her."

"For the last time, that is not who we are," Dr. Flint replied sternly.

A sound came over the loudspeaker, from Sasha's cell. A guttural, mournful sigh that sounded almost inhuman. All eyes turned back to the cell to see Sasha standing, facing them, but seeing only her own ragged reflection in the one-way mirror. She spoke in a low, raspy whisper that sounded both brittle and spiteful, "You know what I want."

Dr. Flint addressed Jake. "She's been asking to speak with you for weeks. You know we've denied her, but time is running out. We need the location of the remaining Hunter bases. I'm concerned that her followers are suffering, afraid; hell, they could even be a danger to themselves or others. We have to get to them. She has repeatedly offered to give us the information, but only if..."

"Only if I speak with her." Jake got the picture.

"It's completely up to you, Jake."

Ben chimed in, "Lives are at stake; that's the point."

Jake could not tear his eyes away from the haunting figure in the cell. He sighed.

* * *

A basic metal chair had been placed in front of the Plexiglas cell. It was all very *Silence of the Lambs.*

Jake entered the room, Sasha on the left, a wall-sized mirror on the right. He knew everyone would be watching this exchange, recording it. *What the hell could she possibly want with me...besides my death?*

Sasha stood motionless, watching Jake's approach through the strands of her thrashed hair. He took a seat, facing her. She sat on the cement floor directly in front of him, her arms wrapped around her knees as she rocked slightly back and forth.

Jake could see her striking beauty through her disheveled surface. The self-inflicted wounds she'd been so arrogantly proud of had all healed over. Her cheek, neck, and wrists, all looked mostly scar-free. Gone was her passion, her devilish grin, the fire in her eyes. Even though she was only in her mid-thirties, she appeared so much older now.

The two sat and stared at each other. The silent awkwardness grew until Jake could hear his own heartbeat.

"Jake London, the Savior of the Damned," she uttered. Her statement was surprisingly free of venom. "You've come to see me at last. I was beginning to think you'd forgotten about me. A girl might take that personally."

Jake mustered all his courage. "What do you want?"

She leaned forward, pressing her forehead to the clear wall. Her eyes fixated on the seamless metal box at Jake's feet. Using his gift, Jake had forced Sasha's nanos from her body and commanded them into the box. Phalanx security had sealed the container permanently, eliminating any way to free the nanotech.

Eventually her gaze rose to Jake's eyes. He couldn't maintain eye contact. Even though he'd defeated her, he could still feel her strength, the power within her.

"I was wrong, Jake. I can't believe I didn't see it before. The signs were there; if only I'd been more aware."

Jake forced himself to stay in the chair when all he wanted to do was run for the door.

She pressed on, "All that time trying to control you and use you. So wrong. So wrong. I should have seen it."

She was infuriating. Jake wanted her to get to the point so he could leave. "What are you talking about?"

"You are a god, Jake. You were sent to put us on the right path. To show us how Mechcraft should be—must be—used in this world. I was misguided in my pursuit to end all of us. And this...this maddening isolation is my punishment for blasphemy against you."

Holy shit! She has really lost her mind! Jake was stunned into silence.

Sasha continued to rant, "I'm so sorry, Jake. For everything I put you through. For all of it. I can never take it back. I can never undo the damage. But going forward, I would ask to be your disciple."

Enough of this. Jake stood. "Tell us where the Hunter bases are. You got what you wanted. I came. Let's get this over with."

Her face contorted in confusion. "Didn't you hear what I said?"

"Hunter. Bases. Where are they located?"

"I'm ready to be your student. Teach me. Guide me."

Jake crossed his arms and waited, glaring at her. Sasha's eyes welled up with tears.

"Jake, please. I am accepting this…this penance. I deserve it. But I want to learn. I want to be better. Help me."

He did not see this coming. At all. She was so far gone. "Sasha, the first step is to reveal the location of your bases so we can help the remaining Hunters. Then we'll see." Jake did his best to sound confident.

Sasha sighed in relief. "Yes. Yes. Of course. I will, Jake. Then we'll talk?"

"The locations."

She sighed. "Hollywood. Anaheim. Pasadena."

Ben Donovan's voice cut in over the speaker. "We'll need addresses."

She looked up at the mirror and gave a sarcastic thumbs-up.

"Thank you," Jake said flatly and headed for the door.

"Wait! Jake!" Sasha desperately called after him.

Jake paused and turned.

"You need me, Jake. Just as I need you. What is light without dark? It's hard to be an angel unless you've been a demon first."

Some undertone of her voice pierced his very soul, and he was terrified to discover that he feared his connection with her more than he feared her. Her words resonated within him on a subconscious level, his cognitive mind unable to grasp the thought logically. He felt weak; his knees becoming Jell-o. He spun and exited the room.

She gazed longingly as the door closed behind him.

CHAPTER 2

Jake sat alone in the cafeteria, his lunch untouched on the tray before him. His black uniform, trimmed out with gray and white, allowed him to blend in with the other students and agents, yet he stood out like a piranha in a swimming pool.

Even after three uneventful months, Jake still caught sight of wary glances from his peers. His unique abilities had saved his life and the lives of his loved ones more than once, but at times like this, he wished he was just like everyone else.

Bex Flint snuck up behind him. Her long auburn hair was pulled back into a pony tail, the dark uniform accentuating her porcelain skin and green eyes. Her devious grin widened as she came up on her prey and kissed his neck in a sudden burst of playful aggression.

He jumped, shaken from his thoughts, but laughed immediately to hide his somberness from her. Bex sat across from him, a smile etched on her face as well. She didn't want Jake to worry about her growing anxiety.

Three months had put some distance to the horrors of Jake's mission. Hundreds had died in the process of getting Jake to Phalanx, and too many, Bex knew, had been caused by her. The slain Hunter elites at the safe house, the hundreds of innocents bloodied and twisted in the wreckage of the train Sasha derailed, the Mechcrafters defeated and slaughtered on the battlefield in front of Phalanx...she blamed herself for them all. Her nightmares had only increased, and she often woke in other parts of the building. She'd been able to mask her despair so far, but she was not confident she could keep it up much longer.

"How was training?" she asked casually.

He decided to be honest. "Your dad called me away from class."

"What'd you do now?" she quipped playfully.

"He asked me to speak with Sasha."

That stopped Bex cold. The blood drained from her face, and her hands began to shake. Her mouth went dry. "What for?" she barely managed to utter.

"It was worth it. We got the addresses to the Hunter bases. We can pick up the stragglers now."

She could see his distress, but felt helpless under the weight of her own anxiety.

Jake noted her sudden change and reached across the table and took her shaking hand. He knew their trial had taken a heavy toll on her, but didn't know how, or if he even should approach the subject with her. He just squeezed her hand gently.

Their relationship had blossomed quickly after the Disruption Day battle was over and peace was established. The crisis of the situation had caused their passions to rise faster than either of them expected, and they made love for the first time almost immediately after the dust had settled.

They knew their parents wouldn't approve, even in this modern age. And they had the insight to acknowledge that advancing their love so fast had potential consequences. Were they emotionally ready for this? Sex was a big deal. It brought them closer on so many levels, but wouldn't they be all the more devastated if things somehow didn't work out between them? Not to mention the possible complications for their Mechcraft ability. Their nanotech was so integrated with their cells, hormones, and so on, that Jake sometimes wondered if these emotions would affect how the power worked.

But it was frustrating to ponder all this, and these thoughts were always cast aside once they were in each other's arms. Bex was Jake's first girlfriend, but Bex had had a few boyfriends in the past. She'd only slept with one, however, and that ended horribly. But that ex was so utterly different from Jake, she was not at all concerned about a repeat of that failure.

The joy they shared in each other's arms only seemed to accelerate their bond, and even though chaos had brought them together, it was there they'd found the greatest contentment. It was genuine caring that kept their love growing, and true friendship as well. They confided in each other things they'd never trust to anyone else, and, now, keeping her anxieties hidden from Jake pained her all the more. She just wasn't ready to address it with him, or, indeed, with herself.

"I'm going out there with Trent and Gauntlet to bring them in," said Jake, breaking the silence.

"Wait. Are you sure? Are you ready for that?"

Jake trusted Gauntlet's leader, Grant MacReady, more than most. This once-rival faction had taken Jake into their possession when he was most vulnerable, but instead of exploiting him, they had helped him reach the safety of the Phalanx headquarters and reunite with his parents. Every day the peace and cooperation between the two remaining factions grew stronger.

"More than ready. Do you want to come along?"

Her lips trembled. She could only shake her head.

Jake took a chance. "Maybe getting outside, back in the field, will help you."

She pulled her hand away. "I'm fine. I'm just…I'm too busy with un-brainwashing the Hunters we already have to go out and play with you nerds."

Jake smiled and shrugged. "Okay. Just a thought."

Bex had been placed in charge of the deprogramming of the former Hunter followers, mostly teens themselves. The goal was, hopefully, to integrate them into Phalanx. So far she had been met with great success, despite being understaffed. Her team of five simply wasn't enough. Her father, Dr. Flint, assured her help was coming.

While she took pride in her efforts with the Hunters, she was troubled by her reluctance to get back out in the field. She had practically recoiled from Jake's offer. The old Bex would have jumped at the chance to go on a field mission, and been out the door before anyone knew she was missing. Now, the very thought of using her Mechcraft sent waves of nausea, dizziness, and even terror through her entire being.

She reached for Jake's hand once again. "Look," she said, "I'll get back out there soon."

He empathized with her far more than she could imagine.

"Sure. Whenever you're ready."

* * *

Dr. Flint made his way to the basement of the Phalanx building. His business with Sasha concluded, he now had to fulfill other duties. He glanced back over his shoulder, observed the empty hall, then descended the steps.

Through several locked doors, he finally found himself standing before his nemesis. The dim light cast amorphous, undulating shadows. The thing had reached out to Dr. Flint several months ago. Telepathically, it had scratched and tickled the back of his brain, prying information from his own nanos. He sensed the intrusion and knew exactly where to find the being. Using persuasion and, later, blackmail, it forced him to make decisions and changes he never would have ordinarily.

He stood before the thing, waiting with trepidation. Then came the expected invasion: hot, prickly sensation in his brain. He absorbed the information, the orders. Behind it all was the voice of reason; he wanted to resist, wanted to fight this goddamned thing, but, in the end, he simply couldn't. Lives were at stake; disobedience on his part meant death for loved ones.

Nodding his acknowledgement of the commands, Dr. Flint turned and left as fast as he could.

CHAPTER 3

Sasha's information came too late. A cooperative mission with Phalanx and Gauntlet revealed the Hunter safe houses in Hollywood and Anaheim void of any life. Each home was in disarray; chairs and couches toppled, TV's smashed on the floor, and papers and mess strewn all about. Chaos told a story of violence in these rooms and halls.

"What the hell happened to them?" Trent pondered out loud.

"No bodies, but all kinds of signs of a struggle," Grant began. "Whatever happened, they either up and left or someone hid the bodies. But then why not clean up the mess lying around?"

"Let's jam. Third time's a charm, I hope," finished Trent.

Grant, Trent, and Jake led a team of three Gauntlet soldiers and three Phalanx agents. Having cleared the first two safe houses, they entered the Pasadena location Sasha had given, expecting to find the same result.

The house stood in Old Town Pasadena, nestled among mini-mansions built in California's Craftsman era of the early twentieth century. Ancient trees and generous, lush foliage added layers of privacy to each estate, allowing the team to go unnoticed in the night.

They stalked their way to the front porch of the dark house. A Gauntlet soldier made quick work of the front door, conjuring a slender silver mech, a softly floating tendril, perfectly suited to the lock. After entering and disengaging the mechanism, the nanos slipped back into his palm and the team entered the dwelling silently. No one was surprised to find the living room in a state of mayhem as their flashlights scanned the area.

"Another freakin' ghost town," he grunted in frustration. Trent turned to Jake, "Think maybe Sasha was full of shit?"

"I just don't know. She seemed sincere. I mean, she was almost relieved we were coming to collect her people."

Trent huffed, "Can't trust that bitch."

"Well, *someone* was here, and a struggle took place just like at the other two safe houses."

The soldiers finished their sweep of the downstairs and moved up to the second floor.

Grant said, "We finish here and go back to Sasha."

"Good luck with that," Trent scoffed. "She'll only talk to the rug rat here."

Grant looked over to Jake, inquisitively.

"He's not wrong," Jake murmured.

"Then *you* have to go back in, Jake. Outthink her."

Trent chimed in, "I'd like a crack at her. I'd get her talking."

A soldier rushed down the steps and approached Grant.

"Sir, you've got to see this."

Upstairs, all the soldiers and agents gawked at something in one of the bedrooms. Grant, Trent, and Jake negotiated the crowd and stood equally stunned upon seeing the sight before them.

Smeared and splattered over two walls and most of the ceiling was the blood and silver of a Hunter faction member. Some time had passed; the blood had coagulated and the silver nanos were almost entirely dissolved.

"Jesus," exclaimed Trent.

Jake staggered back, overwhelmed by the horror in front of him. He put his hand to a wall to steady himself.

The body of a young woman in the black Hunter uniform lay crumpled next to a red-soaked bed. She couldn't have been more than twenty, but her shriveled and drawn flesh made her appear an old woman.

Massive gashes covered her face and torso under her shredded clothes. She looked like she'd been attacked by a rabid bear.

Grant was all business and set to work examining the body.

Trent recovered and joined him, noting the large wounds.

"She never had a chance to heal. Whoever did this killed her before her nanos could stitch her back up."

Grant focused on the torso lacerations, jagged and vicious. He shook his head slowly. "These wounds didn't come from an external attack. These are eruptions from inside her. Look how the edges show a bursting out effect."

Trent noted the subtle difference. "Who the hell did this? What kind of freak are we dealing with?" he whispered.

"We need answers," Jake managed to utter, still catching his breath from the shock of the extreme violence before him.

"And I know where to get them," Trent grunted.

* * *

Later, at Phalanx, Grant split from the two young men to report their findings to Dr. Flint. Jake and Trent turned toward their dorm room, but Greg and Tina London headed them off, stern glares piercing the two boys.

"What were you thinking, Jake?" Tina fumed.

"And why did you let him go?" Greg singled out Trent. "Field work? Really? He's fifteen!"

"Sorry. Sorry...I didn't think. It was a simple task, and given what Jake can do..."

"No excuse!" grunted Tina. "This does not happen again."

"Okay, mom," replied Jake, sheepishly. "Sorry."

"We almost lost you once already. Not going through that again."

Greg looked around. "And I'm going to tear Grant a new one, next time I see him."

Jake and Trent looked to one another. They had much to tell them.

CHAPTER 4

Michael Ash prided himself on his persistence. Throughout his thirty-two years, he'd achieved every goal he set for himself. Joining the LAPD and rising to detective had been his crowning achievement. To get here, he'd foregone the typical path of marriage, home and kids, opting, instead, for a few acquaintances, a small apartment, and a thriving career. Romantic relationships never lasted longer than a few months; the poor women inevitably realized they'd always come second to his job, and left him.

Michael kept his hair clipped short, his wardrobe simple, and his life minimalistic. Fewer distractions equaled fewer mistakes. Friends were an afterthought. He'd enjoy the occasional beer with the co-workers or football game with the cousins, but, in the end, he was married to his badge, and everyone knew it.

As a black man, he'd had a harder fight to achieve the status he'd earned. Discrimination still ran rampant in the department, and he'd contended with his fair share of subtle and not-so-subtle racism. Keeping his eye on the prize of detective, and fighting back against those who stood in his way, Michael managed to push past the bullshit, and build a record of achievements to be proud of.

And now, five years into his current Detective position, he found himself stagnating. Success had come easily, and his record of solved cases was approaching legendary status. There simply were no worlds left to conquer. Then, one fateful night, he witnessed something so profound it changed the course of his life and gave him the motivation he so desperately craved.

Three months ago, he found himself in the iconic Roxy night club in West Hollywood, following up on a missing person case. It was an all-ages night, and he was surrounded by teens. Some local punk band was giving him a headache, and he wanted to finish up his interview and get the hell out.

At the bar, to his right, an argument broke out between twins and a late-teen boy and girl. He couldn't make out what was said, but in one instant his entire world shifted. The teen boy produced two small metallic spheres from his palms. He literally *bled* liquid metal through his flesh and conjured the shapes.

Before he could react to the sight before him, the twins bolted and the two teens pursued. Michael gathered his wits and ran after them. He emerged from the club and ran to the right, but froze as he witnessed a street brawl involving nearly a dozen people. Each of them conjuring and attacking with the strange liquid metal.

A dark-haired woman brushed past him and entered the fray, throwing metallic tentacles around the two teens, instantly securing them.

Michael looked at the gathering crowd, many of them filming the event with their phones, and he called for backup.

The woman had the two teens pinned to the ground with more of the strange metallic material. They exchanged words. Though he couldn't make out what was said, the spite etched on their faces spoke volumes.

Then, in a surprise move, the teen boy hurled some weapon at the woman, freeing them from her grip. In a flash they were gone. The woman's companions gathered around her.

Michael began his approach, hand on his holster. He was going to find out what the hell was going on. The sirens blared in the background; the cavalry was almost here.

The woman barked some orders and her companions spread into a line at her sides, facing the growing crowd in front of the Roxy. Michael took position and drew his weapon.

"Freeze! LAPD. Don't move."

The companions obeyed, and raised their arms. Michael moved in slowly. Something flashed past him. An object sliced his gun barrel clean off. Before he could react, Michael heard the screams behind him. He turned to the crowd to see more than a dozen phones drop to the ground, their owners clutching their hands. Likewise, nearby security cams tore and sparked, the sound of wrenching metal piercing the night air. People screamed and jumped in surprise as Michael spun back around to the cause of the damage, but the woman and her companions were gone.

The authorities arrived and the interviews began, but, later it was discovered that all files, data, video, audio from the dozens of phones and cameras present were corrupted. No video or photographic evidence of the incident existed.

Michael knew at that moment his life would never be the same.

Now, obsessed with finding these people, he poured over endless hours of video from street cams and security cams on dates and incidents that seemed suspicious. Most of the data amounted to nothing, but a few clips spurred his curiosity further.

In particular, the LA Blue Line train platform terrorist attack and subsequent derailment three months ago perplexed him. Surrounding cameras and onboard security had somehow captured nothing. Of the platform attack, dozens of people gave the same account of the slaughter of uniformed men and women right in front of them, yet the area betrayed no evidence of violence of any kind. And later, at the derailed train wreckage, no cause could be found that would send the train off its tracks. Over one hundred people lost their lives, and no cause could be found.

Michael knew what he'd seen. He knew these people harnessed some power beyond anything he or anyone had ever heard of before. He considered and rejected theories about aliens. No, this was science. This was man-made tech.

Whatever the source, he felt compelled to discover the truth.

CHAPTER 5

The night seemed to encroach upon them as Jake and Trent drove to their destination. Jake felt the change in the air. A murderer roamed the streets, a killer who knew what they were and how to rip the life from them. The atmosphere felt claustrophobic.

He hated going behind his parents' backs, but there was so much at stake here. Although he was just a novice, he recognized his unique ability made him an asset to this investigation.

Near midnight, they turned down side streets in the South Bay area, about fifteen miles south of Los Angeles. Jake recognized the warehouses and knew exactly where they were headed. They parked in front of a nondescript warehouse. A full parking lot was the only thing that distinguished this building from the others.

In moments they were inside. The underground Mechcrafter fight club hadn't changed since the last time Jake had visited. Seeing the caged arena made him wince, recalling the beat down he took at the hands of a thirteen-year-old girl. The miniature Harley Quinn had completely kicked his ass—to the delight of the crowd.

At this late hour, only about fifty patrons watched and cheered on the bouts in the arena. Mechcrafters who had turned away from joining any faction had found a refuge in this place, a welcome reprieve from the mean streets.

Trent motioned for Jake to follow, and they made their way to the bar. Trent smiled, recognizing the same bartender from whom he'd milked info on their mission with Jake.

Trent rushed up to the unsuspecting bartender and sucker punched him in the face. The thin, prickly man collapsed, and Trent hopped the bar to join his target. Jake ran up, shocked by Trent's move.

Trent conjured a mech, commanded it into a thick collar, and mentally willed it to clamp around the bartender's neck. The mech lifted the gasping man back to a standing position.

"Remember me, asshole? You sold us out to the Hunters."

"What?" he gasped. "I would never—"

The mech collar tightened at Trent's command, cutting off the poor bastard's speech.

"Jake here told me he wants to rip your head off," lied Trent.

Jake's eyes went wide. Trent winked at him secretly. "But I convinced him to just maim you instead."

"Pl-please," the man could barely get the words out.

"I don't know, man," Trent replied playfully. "Once he gets a taste for the violence, there's no holding him back."

Jake understood his part in this ruse, and played it up for Trent. "Back off, Trent," he hissed. "He's mine!"

"N...no! No!" the scruffy man begged.

"Sorry, buddy, I can't control this kid."

"I can't control it, Trent! I have to do it."

"God, no. No. Please!"

Jake did his best rage-fueled Hulking-out performance, building it to a crescendo. All the while the bartender's terror grew and his eyes widened. At the height of the man's panic, Jake focused his unique power and forced the jerk's own nanos to come forth from his torso, through the flesh, to form two, thin writhing tentacles.

Seeing his own nanos active without his command was too much for the bartender. Tears flowed and he was on the verge of passing out, when Jake commanded the tentacles to curve to either side of the man's core and begin tickling him vigorously.

Snot flew from the terrified bartender's nose as he let out involuntary bursts of laughter and screams to create a strange mix worthy of the best EDM DJ's craft. He wiggled and fought against the assault but could not withstand it.

Trent released the mech collar, letting the nanos absorb back into his skin. He didn't hide his disappointment.

"Really Jake?" he smirked. "Tickling? This son-of-a-bitch led Sasha right to our safe house. This is the best you could come up with?"

"I think it has a certain comic aesthetic."

The bartender, still crying, fell to his knees.

"Goddamnit, Jake. Enough of this shit."

"You sure? Alright."

He released the tentacles, which dissolved to liquid and fled back into the man's body, but Jake was far from finished. He knew all too well what this man's betrayal had caused and had no plans to play nice. Telepathically, he seized control of the bartender's nanos again.

Suddenly, the man gasped and clutched his throat, gagging as his own nanos filled his throat and lungs, drowning him in liquid metal.

Trent stopped and stared in horror. "Holy shit." Shaking himself from awe, he leaned down and grabbed the bartender's shirt tight.

"You're going to tell me everything I need to know, or Jake really will end you."

The choking man managed a panicked nod. Jake released him and took a seat at the bar. The bartender gasped and hacked for a long while.

Trent looked the disheveled the man in the eye. "What do you know about recent Mechcrafter deaths?" His eyes revealed he knew plenty, and Trent would get it out of him.

"I don't know, man. There's...talk. People say shit."

"Tell me," Trent leaned in closer.

The bartender put his hand up in a protective gesture. "Word is it's just one person, not a faction. People assumed it was the Hunters, but then Hunters started dying too."

"How many have been killed?"

"No one knows for sure. Maybe ten. Maybe a dozen."

"And no one can identify him?"

"I don't know, man. Only one girl escaped so far."

"Who is it?"

"Her," he replied, motioning to the caged arena. Skipping playfully around her fallen enemy was the young girl who had humiliated Jake those months ago. Sporting her trademark pig tails, she danced around a large man who had fallen to his knees, dazed from whatever assault she had just delivered.

"Aw hell," muttered Jake, feeling a twinge of memory pain in his groin.

"When did all this start?" Trent refocused.

The bartender looked nervously to Jake. "About the time *he* showed up."

CHAPTER 6

Bex gave up trying to sleep. Jake and Trent were still out rounding up Hunter stragglers, and with each hour her concern grew. Her intuition was in full red alert. She had no immediate reason for her anxiety, but she couldn't fight the nagging feeling something wasn't right.

Of course she could text them, but she fought the urge. Instead she'd let them work their mission.

She left her room, leaving her roommate sleeping peacefully. Wandering the quiet halls and courtyard, she found herself in the library, drawn by a light where there should be none. She already suspected who she'd find.

Sure enough, Artemis Whitaker sat a table engrossed in what his tablet was showing him. Thin, but with a round face, Artemis smiled wide when he saw Bex enter. He was a young fifteen, not yet come into his age. His dark skin still held the smoothness of pre-adolescence. He kept his hair conservatively short.

"Bex!" he exclaimed. "What are you doing here?"

She took a seat across from him. "I could ask you the same."

"I fell into the 'just-one-more-chapter' trap."

"As usual," she smiled. Bex suspected this kid was a genius and had great potential. Plus he was just about the friendliest person she knew. Unfortunately, not everyone saw Artemis the way she did.

The kid had been bullied for much of his life, and his spirit had been nearly broken. His father, David, was not a Mechcrafter, but held high enough office in the government to warrant a favor from Dr. Flint. A few handshakes later, Artemis was offered the Mechcraft injection and a new life. David had hoped this new ability would give his son the confidence and protection he needed and provide a way for him to make a real difference in the world.

Things didn't go as planned. Sure enough, at age fourteen, Artemis endured the horrifying conversion process that unleashed and activated the nanotech in the adolescent body. He recovered, but had been unable to summon forth a single mech since that initial burst. Not a sphere, nor blade, nor shield, not even a pebble.

So, even in the safety of the Phalanx headquarters, bullying began anew, making his life hell all over again. Until the day Jake arrived. Jake, also an outcast much of his life, took to Artemis immediately, feeling a kinship with him. As soon as word got out that the wildcard, Jake, the most feared person in all of Mechcraftdom, had befriended Artemis Whitaker, he became untouchable. The bullying ceased.

Bex squirted Lemonade-scented hand sanitizer into her palm and rubbed her hands together. "Any change in your 'problem'?"

"Sore subject," he responded in rapid-fire. "Logically I should be much farther along, yet the conjuring eludes me. I have studied nearly every tome in the Mechcraft archives. Every article. Every memoir. I even explored classified documents. Nothing has helped."

"Classified?" she perked up.

"Please don't tell your dad. I meant no harm. I'm just desperate. Am I hopeless?"

"Come on, Artemis. It will happen for you. It's different for each of us."

"My brain agrees with your assessment, but my heart has doubts."

"I've heard of people receiving the injections and having their nanos fail, but it's extremely rare. Have faith that you'll figure this out. There really is no rush."

"Maybe not, but, still, I'd like the means of defending myself without relying on the assistance of others."

"Nothing wrong with leaning on friends, Artemis."

"One would like to think it goes both ways, and until the day comes when I can also be relied upon, I shall persevere. Nose to the books and all."

"Maybe that's part of the problem. Learning the academics is fine, but you need to dive into the artistic side of Mechcraft. The feelings, the emotions." Bex rose and strolled to the door. "Let's get you into the training room. Leave the books alone for awhile."

"If you think that will help my cause, I'll try anything."

"Tomorrow we start."

She waved as she opened the door.

"Bex," he called. "One last thing."

"Yes?"

"Have you ever heard of 'Project Ares'?"

"Aries? The zodiac sign?"

"No, the Greek god of war, Ares."

"Um, I don't think so. Why? What is it?"

"I came across references to Project Ares in some of the documents I borrowed."

"Classified docs, you mean."

"Regretfully, yes."

"Well, what is this Project Ares?"

"That's just it; twelve separate references to it in printed communications between Phalanx and Washington, but no details on what it is."

"Clearly it's above our pay grade and none of our business. Have a good night, Artemis." Bex gave another wave and was gone.

Artemis started to close his book, but became distracted by the page, and simply returned to studying.

CHAPTER 7

"How's your balls?" asked the girl as she stuffed food truck fries into her mouth.

It had been easy to get her to leave the Mechcraft fight club. The promise of food was all it took to get her to come along. She looked underweight. Trent wondered how long it had been since she'd had a meal.

"Just fine, no thanks to you," Jake shot back, still feeling the phantom pain.

"Sorry, dude. I had to give 'em a good show. No hard feelings?"

"Just tell us what you know, and we'll call it even." Trent slid a tray stacked high with a thick bacon cheeseburger across the picnic table closer to the young girl.

The park they dined in fell into the newer, trendy efforts by the city to build community. Everything was clean, well-maintained, and lit with string after string of antique looking Edison bulbs. A nearby pond soothed the mild crowd by providing lower temperatures and relaxing water sounds.

Five gourmet food trucks parked in a row at a park not far from the clandestine club, each fronted by a long line of hungry business suits and Pilates students. Dog owners and joggers rounded out the mix of people around. Even at this late hour, Los Angeles bustled.

Jake pondered their ignorance to the hidden world all around and found himself envious. They would go about their daily lives of Starbucks, Netflix binging, and nights out with friends, oblivious to the war that raged under their very noses.

"Look, dude. I'll tell you what I know, but you aren't going to believe it."

Jake snapped back to the task at hand.

"So, Princess Badass...you got a name?" asked Trent, smiling.

"Sophie," she quipped, "and you are Trent and Jake."

Jake leaned forward. "How did you—"

"Come on. Everybody knows who you are," she laughed. "You can do some wicked shit with your 'Craft. And your little hive ended the Hunters. Yay for the good guys, I guess."

Jake's curiosity distracted him from their course. He asked, "Why do you choose not to have a faction? Wouldn't you feel safer if—"

"Let me stop you right there, Johnny Wildcard," she cut in. "Save your speech. You'll never get me to join a faction. I don't take sides, I don't join causes. Whatever sales pitch you have in your damaged brain, just spare me."

Trent took control of the conversation. "Fine. go it alone, then. We just came to find out who's murdering Mechcrafters. This affects all of us. All factions. All indies, all weird little girls. We need to catch this maniac."

Sophie sighed. Her thirteen year old frame slumped slightly. She knew these guys wouldn't believe her story. No one did. "Yeah. Good luck with that. You're gonna need it."

"Just...what does he look—"

"Okay, look. I didn't see much. He's big. Moves super fast, I mean, I've never seen anything like it. Took out three of my friends like they were made of paper. Punched holes in them, *through* them."

All three sat silent. Sophie took a massive bite of burger, her slurps interrupting the quiet.

Trent found his voice first. "Killed them all before anyone could fight back?"

Through her burger chewing she said, "Told you. You don't believe me."

"Listen, spark plug, are you absolutely sure about this?" Trent pushed.

"Dude. I barely got out of there."

Jake, not sure if she was full of shit or not, asked, "How did you escape?"

She put the burger down, drank some Coke, and added sadly, "Leta, my...friend. Last second before it killed her, she shot me with her mech. Hit me in the chest and sent me out the window. I fell five stories, but saved myself with a twist landing, last second. I ran as far and fast as I could. She saved me, and I heard her screams as she died. She saved me."

Trent eyed her, judging her face and body language. "I believe you," he simply stated.

Both Jake and Sophie looked at him incredulously.

Keeping his gaze fixed on Sophie, he added, "I think you should come back to Phalanx with us. We'll keep you—"

"Safe? That's a laugh. *Omae*, aren't you listening? No one is safe. Last thing I want is a gang. I keep low and quiet and fast, this asshole won't find me. I hang out with you guys and the dorks at Phalanx, I'm as good as dead. Screw that."

* * *

Michael Ash sat across from the chief, a large desk between them. Chief Darryl Higgins leaned back and tapped his pen on the edge of the desk, as he always did. Michael had been through this before, and found these meetings a complete waste of time.

He had just recovered one sliver of video from an office security camera, somehow missed when every other camera had been destroyed. The video captured the bizarre scene from that impactful night from between two buildings, so barely any of the incident appeared on the footage, but it did hold one excellent shot of the woman's face. It was enough to keep him going.

He'd been about to bring to bear all the tech the LAPD offered to find her, and then Higgins had interrupted the whole thing. Sitting across from his condescending stare grated on his nerves.

"This ends now," grumbled Higgins. "Your case load is stacking up. You aren't following up on your open files. The incident at the Roxy is a dead end. Do not spend another minute on it."

"When have I ever let you down before? Trust me, I'll keep my cases maintained like I always do."

"Your track record is the only thing keeping you from suspension."

After the humiliating meeting with the chief, Michael had put himself in front of the LAPD facial matching database. Once he'd obtained a fairly clear image of the woman, he'd spent a week at the machine searching for a match. If this woman had ever been arrested, her picture would show up. On a national scale, the search was slow-going, but Michael had the patience, the persistence to see it through.

This power they wielded. It was dangerous, potentially a terrorist threat. *Who the hell were these people?*

CHAPTER 8

Jake, Bex, and Trent sat alone in the cafeteria. The coffee was poured, the eggs, bacon, and toast served up, but none of them had touched their breakfast. They had filled Bex in on the events of the previous night; now it seemed no one had an appetite.

They had slipped back in, updated Dr. Flint, and gone to bed without being caught by the observant parents. But being grounded was the least of Jake's concerns now.

"Have you told my dad?" she asked.

"Woke him up. We couldn't sit on info like this," Trent replied.

"It was weird," added Jake.

"Weird how?"

Jake continued, "He seemed distracted. Didn't really care."

"He was just so casual about it. Said he'd take care of it, and ushered us out."

"Maybe he was just tired. Half awake," Bex replied, a bit too defensively.

"Yeah, whatever. It was just strange is all," finished Trent.

"I'll talk to him," reassured Bex.

Artemis approached with his tray of breakfast foods. "May I join you?"

Jake scooted over. "Artemis, you don't have to ask. Just sit with us."

"Yeah, Arty. You're one of the crew now." Trent gave his plate a wry smile. Jake sensed Trent wasn't fully on board with having Artemis around all the time. He didn't understand.

"Thank you," he was barely able to mask his enthusiasm. "What is the topic for discussion today?"

They all looked at one another. The unspoken conversation: *Do we bring him in on this?*

"Just the investigation from last night," Bex tried to be casual.

"Do tell. Did you learn anything new? Cracked the case?"

"We've made some headway, but can't really talk about it," Trent quipped.

Artemis just smiled, happy to be part of the group. "With Holmes and Watson on the case, I'm sure it'll be solved in no time."

Bex pivoted quickly. "Artemis is going to get in some gym time. Try to get over his...issue."

"Not a bad idea, kid," agreed Trent.

"Who's your trainer?" asked Jake.

"Well," he began, "I was hoping one of you might step up to the challenge."

"Sorry, Artemis. I'm still on deprogramming Hunter duty," answered Bex, not wanting to confess her trepidation at conjuring any mechs at this point. Instead, she gave Trent a subtle nod towards Artemis. "But I have someone even better in mind."

"I'm new to this too; I can't train anyone," said Jake looking directly at Trent, who only rolled his eyes.

"Why not," he sighed. "Alright, Arty, it's you and me, *Rocky*-style."

"Ah yes, 'Adrienne!'" he added, doing his best Rocky Balboa impersonation.

All three sat silent. It was terrible.

"Never do that again," Trent scowled.

* * *

Bex entered Dr. Flint's office. Dad was busy at the laptop, as usual.

"Hello, dear. What can I do for you?"

"Hi dad," she took a seat across from him. "What did you think of the news Trent gave you last night?"

"They told you what happened? I guess I shouldn't be surprised."

"Of course they did. So? What are your thoughts and what is the plan?"

He seemed distracted by the laptop screen. "It's under control, Rebecca. We've got people on it."

"Good. Who is this guy? Why is he doing this?"

"Our people are checking into it. Isn't Tina London expecting you in the History of Mechcraft class right now?"

"So, does that mean you won't tell me what's going on?"

"It's classified. You know the rules."

She was taken aback by his sterile attitude. He was usually so warm. She didn't like this. "Dad, I get it. But we've always been able to share details. That's our deal. I tell you embarrassing teen stuff, and you tell me classified government secrets."

"Yes, yes. All true," he smiled, "but...I'm sorry, Rebecca. This is just one case I cannot discuss with anyone. Now if you'll excuse me, I have Washington on my back at the moment." He directed his focus back to the laptop and began typing away.

Bex slowly stood, unsure what to make of this conversation. Exasperated, she simply left the office without another word, and was stung when he didn't acknowledge her exit.

CHAPTER 9

A large mech sphere, the size of a bowling ball, struck Artemis in the chest, knocking him flat on his back.

Trent recalled his nanos to his skin and gave the kid a hand back to his feet. "You're supposed to conjure up a shield and block it."

"Yes, that is a good strategy, and definitely what I had intended."

"I see we've really got our work cut out for us."

"Am I a lost cause?"

"No one's a lost cause, Arty. Just need to unfold the map, find your course. Not try to be what everyone else expects you to be."

Smirks from other Mechcrafters echoed in the large training room. Other teens had stopped their activities upon seeing the struggling craftless Mechcrafter. He had heard it all. Sexual innuendo, calling his manhood into question, jokes comparing the number of his friends to his I.Q., the whole juvenile gambit.

"Ignore those assholes," Trent said, flipping them all off. "One day you'll be able to kick all their asses. Or better yet, you'll be so rich and powerful you can pay others to kick their asses. Let's try again."

Trent stepped back a dozen feet and faced Artemis. "You just need to get out of your head. You're thinking too much."

"I've been told that."

"Look, it's more of an emotional thing."

"I don't know what that means."

Trent pondered for a moment. "Think of it as desire. You want that girl. You want that shiny new car, or, well, that mega processor. You will do anything to make it happen."

"I want to excel in my studies and graduate Valedictorian."

"Well, okay. whatever floats your boat, I guess. It's the *wanting* that is key. Picture yourself achieving that goal. Close your eyes. Picture it."

Artemis complied and closed his eyes, unable to quiet the hope and fear he felt.

"Now focus that desire; picture the nanos coming out of your skin. See them obeying your commands. Need it. Crave it."

Artemis focused, held his hand at chest level, palm up.

"Now make it happen," finished Trent, revealing his own hope for the kid.

At first nothing happened. Moments passed and the giggles from the jerks were the only sounds in the chamber.

Then all eyes went to Artemis' hand. Nanos were bleeding through the skin, coating the palm. The liquid silver overflowed and dripped to the floor.

"Open your eyes, Arty."

Artemis was amazed at the sight before him. Nanos at last! His smile stretched from ear to ear. "I don't believe it! I'm doing it—I'm really doing it!"

"It's all you, kid. Now command it to make something."

"Like what?"

"Anything. Use your imagination."

Artemis focused, and the nanos in his hand stirred. A small, thin tendril began to rise from the pool.

Trent found himself far more excited than he expected to be.

In an instant the tendril and all the liquid metal exploded into a chaotic mess and then fled back into Artemis' skin, knocking him back a step.

"What happened?" asked Trent.

"I—I don't know."

"Well, I still call it a win."

* * *

Tears flowed from the eyes of the former Hunter followers. Five of them sat in chairs weeping openly. They were arranged in a circle with two Mechcrafters seated facing them. The Hunters finally had a breakthrough today. It was never easy to accept the truth of what you were and had done. And so it was with this group.

Bex and Neera Bahar, her closest female friend, looked to each other with victorious tears in their own eyes. They had successfully deprogrammed another group of former killers duped by Sasha's diabolical brainwashing.

Adults, experts in psychology, sociology, and modern cultism were with them. They did the heavy lifting in all this. But Bex and Neera were peers. These Hunters related to them on a level the adults could never achieve. So it fell upon them to help these former enemies to see the error of their ways and start anew.

Neera had been like an older sister to Bex when they were growing up among the faction. They often stayed together at Neera's, staying up all night, creating entire puppet shows using their newly acquired tech, and sharing every secret. As they matured, Neera had encouraged Bex to think of herself as absolutely special, and had even served, occasionally, as a surrogate mother. The only thing Neera had kept to herself was her growing affection for Trent.

She was seventeen now, and ready to take on the world. Her father, Shandir, had taught her well. Five years ago, her own mother had been killed in the field, and her murderer had never been caught. All they knew was that it was a Hunter. Assigning Neera to deprogram the very people who were responsible for her mother's death was no random decision, no oversight. Shandir had insisted.

And he'd been right. Having Bex next to her gave her courage, and this arduous process had turned out to be therapeutic for Neera, cathartic. She had been able to let go of so much rage seeing these poor bastards wake up from their own nightmares. And she took pride that she was a part of it.

The sobbing slowed and the hugs followed. The gratitude in their eyes was unforgettable. As was the sorrow and regret.

As Neera and Bex dried their own tears and hugged, adult Mechcrafters escorted the Hunter subjects out. The deprogrammed would be taken to new housing. No more cells, but for now, they'd still be staying separate from the Phalanx students and would remain under watchful eyes until they further proved the deprogramming had truly taken hold.

From there it was a chance at a new life. Adults could work for Phalanx at one of the facilities across the country, and the teens could become students of Phalanx and learn their ways and methods.

So far, so good.

Only one problem: Bex was on the verge of a nervous breakdown, and no one, not even Jake knew just how close she was. Her PTSD over the events three months ago grew worse every day. She still managed to hold on to the professional façade and the ability to work with these former Hunters, but she felt her defenses cracking.

Neera, however, had sensed her friend slipping for weeks now, but Bex was always in denial. Neera had even gone to Dr. Flint behind Bex's back to implore him to give them extra hands to help with the deprogramming, as she could feel the strain taking its toll. Neera herself was exhausted as well. A handful of adults and teens handling so much responsibility was ridiculous. They had deprogrammed a solid forty-five Hunters now, but almost two hundred remained. It was not a fast process, especially with the deprogrammers themselves caught up in dealing with their own fallout.

As the former Hunters left the room, she had a few minutes to give Bex the good and bad news she'd just received from Dr. Flint. Bex was not going to be happy.

Both girls took deep, cleansing breaths, recovering from the intense emotions of the session. Neera pulled her long black hair back into a ponytail and steeled herself for the conversation. She was tall and slender, and carried herself as an imposing force to be reckoned with.

Bex took notice when Neera's demeanor diminished and she slouched a bit.

"What's wrong?" she asked.

No way to avoid this. Bex had to be told. "I have some news. Your dad's sending in some reinforcements for this deprogramming. A family of three to help take the load off our shoulders." Neera had spent a few young years in London and still carried a slight British accent. It gave her voice a soothing, lyrical quality.

"That's great. About damn time. When will they start? Who is it?"

"They are considered experts in dealing with this kind of thing," she continued. "They are being sent in from Washington, DC."

Bex's expression shifted from joy to dread. "Don't tell me."

"I'm afraid so, Bex."

"Dante Barnes," she hissed. "Fuck."

* * *

"So who the hell is Dante Barnes?" asked Jake at dinner. Bex had given him the news that help was coming for the deprogramming, and had dropped the bomb of Dante as well.

"He's my ex."

That gave Jake pause: *Why should I be worried?* The look on Bex's face made him doubt his confidence. "Well, I mean, I guess that's okay. If he's an expert then he can really help make things go easier for you, right?"

"It ended badly, Jake. Real bad. My father doesn't even know. Now I wish I'd told him so he wouldn't be bringing him back here."

"Bad like how? You're worrying me."

"He's used to getting what he wants, okay? And when I wanted to break up, he disagreed. It got ugly."

"What the hell? Did he hit you?"

"Worse. We actually fought. Battled with our mechs. It was away from here; no one knows it happened. I had to end it with him, but he wouldn't hear me. He stalked me for weeks, but being here in this place, there was just no escaping him."

"I can't believe he attacked you."

"He didn't, not exactly. We took it outside, met in an alley nearby. I asked him one last time to let me go. He laughed and said he'd never give up on me. I was so sick of the spying. Sick of the manipulations. Sick of the pressures. He said he'd never quit; I honestly thought I'd never be rid of him."

She fought hard against an emotional outburst. *Not here. Not in front of the students and faculty.* Jake took her hand. It trembled.

"What happened?" he asked cautiously.

"I went nuts, drew mechs on him. Then he did the same. It was terrible, brutal. In the end, I'd...I nearly killed him. I got him back to Phalanx and into the hospital." Bex sat, looking at her hands, holding back tears. She took a rough breath. "I told them Hunters had ambushed us. When he woke, he didn't deny that story. He didn't rat me out. His family transferred to the DC office and I never saw him again."

"Jesus. How long ago was this?"

"About two years now."

"Oh my god, that's all? This is still a fresh wound! And now he's coming back. Shit, we have to stop this. We gotta get your dad to cancel the order."

"No. That would mean telling him the truth. I can't do that."

"So you'd rather deal with this psycho coming back into your life?"

"No, but I—I just don't know what else to do."

"We have to tell your dad."

"Absolutely not, Jake. I'm ashamed of myself. I couldn't bear to see his face, hearing what I've done."

"Bex, it was self-defense."

"No, I attacked first. I almost killed him. We're leaving this alone. We'll deal with Dante when he comes."

Trent and Artemis sat down at the table, trays of pasta in hand.

"Wait till you hear what happened," said Trent. He looked at the strained awkwardness on their faces.

"What did we miss?"

CHAPTER 10

The Gauntlet faction headquarters rested secretly, deep below the Los Angeles industrial area, a mile south of the Convention Center and the LA Live complex of restaurants and concert venues.

Hundreds of feet below an empty warehouse, a small army of Mechcrafters lived out their calling in a faction war that no regular human knew about. Their commander, Grant MacReady, maintained a fierce loyalty in his soldiers. They trusted him and would follow him into any battle, regardless of the odds.

That was before the end of the war. Three months ago, the Hunter faction was utterly decimated, and a genuine peace now existed between Gauntlet and Phalanx. At first, it had been a time to rejoice, a time to rest and rethink.

However, since then, complacency had become the enemy. With no missions and no cause to champion, the soldiers had grown anxious, bored, and leaned into conspiracy theories. Doubt crept insidiously into the minds of some of the Gauntlet soldiers.

The job of tracking down straggler Hunters was not particularly fulfilling, certainly not enough to keep the troops occupied. In-fighting was becoming a problem, and with it, trust was diminishing.

Grant could feel it all around, but he felt powerless against it. He'd given his faction everything they had wanted, and now, without external prey, they attacked each other.

His counsel, Timothy James and Bea Moreno, were little help and argued between them. While Bea was a staunch supporter of building a new, peace-time community, Timothy grew more distant and non-communicative every day.

He sat across from them in the war room, listening to them argue over the next moves for their faction.

"We simply cannot trust Phalanx. Sooner or later they will impose their will on us. They have the backing of the government. How long before DC makes demands of fealty from us?" barked Timothy.

"And would it be so bad to be back in the fold?" argued Bea. "We'd have legitimacy again. Funding again."

"Are you kidding? And be under their thumb? Our every move scrutinized and called into question? No thank you."

"What would you have us do then?"

"Separate from them."

Bea scoffed.

"I mean it," Timothy continued. "Separate, but remain at peace, of course."

Grant leaned forward to address them. "And what about this new development?"

Timothy laughed. "A Mechcraft serial killer? It's a joke. Lies from a discontented underground."

"How can you be so sure?" he pressed.

"Come on, Grant. You know it's bullshit. Why are you giving it any thought? It's just a psycho Mechcrafter or two out there picking off stragglers. Let Phalanx handle it if they want."

"Our kind are being slaughtered, Timothy."

"Fine.... Fine. I do agree that it gives our soldiers something constructive to do. They're bored and frustrated enough."

"We need to discuss long-term goals for Gauntlet. You are both correct in your arguments. Continued contact and dealings with Phalanx will cause more interference from Washington at some point, but it will also give us access and funds and missions for the soldiers," Grant stated.

"What are you proposing, then?" asked Bea.

"It's going to sound extreme. It's going to sound radical. But I think this may be the only way to thrive, moving forward. I'm considering a full merge with Phalanx, becoming one faction again."

Bea's jaw dropped and Timothy was visibly shaken. His face went from shock to rage, and he slammed his fist to the table.

"You're crazy! This is madness. You can't be serious."

"It solves all our problems. Think about it. We'd no longer be the outsiders drawing the all-seeing eye of Washington to us. We'd have one hundred percent access to all things in the Mechcraft world. We'd have strengthened numbers. We'd have legitimate missions again; ways we can actually help people."

"I have to say," began Bea, "I'm with Timothy on this. I don't think you've thought this through, Grant, or how the troops are going to react to the idea."

"It would be full scale mutiny. Or desertion. No, this can't happen. There has to be another way," exclaimed Timothy.

"I'm fighting for our future. I'm playing the long-game. You two need to ponder what's at stake here and then get on board. We have to show a united front when we tell the soldiers."

"Whoa. '*When?*' What happened to 'if?'" prodded Timothy.

* * *

Jake and Bex simply couldn't keep their hands off each other. Their lovemaking brought them peace in the midst of all the chaos in their lives, and encouraged their love to grow.

In Jake's bed, he held her as she rested her head on his chest. Her curves pressed against him, and he found himself lost in her beauty.

As he caressed her arm draped over his torso, he thought about how lucky he was that fate had put them together. There were times he hated having Mechcraft, resented all the dangers it held. But with Bex, he could face any struggle, any hardship.

And now he knew she needed him. Her PTSD had grown in severity. Even though she avoided talking about it, he could tell that she was barely keeping herself together.

"I love you," she whispered. His heart sped up, for he'd been wanting to say those words for weeks.

"I love you too," he said. "More than words can say."

She smiled and said, "I've been wanting to say it to you for a long time now."

"Same here."

She giggled. "We are so barfy."

"Yeah. The worst," he laughed.

He had wanted to broach the topic of her PTSD, but now, in this moment, he could only enjoy this major leap forward in their relationship. There would be another time to discuss nervous breakdowns and psycho ex-boyfriends. He was content simply to hold her in his arms.

* * *

Artemis had dealt with a plethora of bullies in his lifetime. Most scenarios merely descended into name-calling humiliations. It was rare that any jerk got physical with him. So it struck him as ironic that this place of supposed safety and protection, Phalanx, would deliver him to the worst bullies he ever had the displeasure of meeting.

Rick, Jonas, Mark, and Chloe pummeled him with small mech pellets, some hammer mech strikes to his torso, and an endless barrage of humiliating verbal insults.

They'd caught him alone in the training room after hours. No escape. No protectors. As he lay on the floor in the fetal position, taking the hits, he wondered why he was so constantly targeted. What had he done in his life to justify this torment and punishment?

Rick, the leader of the pack, was a husky kid of seventeen with the mentality and maturity of a nine year old. Between fart jokes and small animal abuse, he was destined to be a cancer on society. The faculty, however, was unaware of the extent of his psychosis, and so he had, thus far, gotten away with all manner of evil deeds.

Jonas, sixteen, thin, lanky, and awkward, was the brains. He let Rick believe he was the leader, but Jonas made all the decisions. Coming from a Wall Street financial family, he was ruthless, raised on cutthroat tactics and praise for crushing enemies.

Mark just wanted to be accepted. He weaseled his way into this group by obeying whatever demented task they set him to. He earned their approval on the backs of the innocent kids he tormented. He was fifteen, almost invisibly average. He desperately wanted to be part of something; he didn't much care where the moral compass fell.

Then there was Chloe. Sixteen and already hardness was etched onto her otherwise pretty face. On paper, she was amazing: high marks on all the tests, social etiquette was on point around the adults, Mechcraft talent ranked in the top five percent, and she came from a loving home. No one could pinpoint where it all went wrong simply because none of the adults in her life had a clue how conniving, manipulative, and abusive she'd turned out to be. Hell, even these boys, who believed they were in control, were merely pawns for her. The icing on the cake for Chloe was the absolute idolization of Sasha. Not for her masochistic desire to end all Mechcrafters, no. Chloe admired Sasha's power and her lack of hesitation or fear to seize what she wanted. Chloe was actually crushed over Sasha's defeat and demise.

The bullies had been so enraptured of their handiwork against Artemis, they hadn't noticed a young student witness their deeds and run for help.

"Get it through your head, you don't belong here," barked Rick.

"Can't even conjure up a nugget. Pathetic," laughed Chloe.

Jonas lighted up. "Maybe we should make an example out of him! You know, to scare away any other wannabes from even thinking of joining us."

"Yeah! Like what are you thinking?" asked Mark eagerly.

Jonas pondered, then snapped his fingers. "I know. We'll go medieval on him. Draw and Quarter him."

The others looked on in dismay. Jonas sighed, frustrated having to explain history to these dolts. "We wrap mechs around each limb and pull in four different directions till he rips apart. Come on, you guys!"

They exploded with excitement. Even Chloe, who found the idea beneath her, still wanted to see how it would play out.

In moments, each had summoned a vine or tentacle mech, wrapped it securely around Artemis' wrists and ankles, and had pulled it tight, though not to the point of pain—not yet. Just getting into the scare phase.

And Artemis was damned terrified. Fear raced through him like never before. No one was coming to save him. He was alone and he was helpless. He fought back tears. Sobbing would only give them what they wanted. He could hang on to this one last bit of resistance. Deny them the show.

"Come on, Fartemis," yelled Rick. "I know you wanna cry!"

"Stop trying to be brave. It's just us here," coaxed Chloe.

"Stop talking. Let's do this!" yelled Mark and immediately commanded his mech to pull.

The others followed suit, and Artemis found himself lifted off the floor, each limb on fire from the pain. He cried out, unable to hold it in. He squeezed his eyes shut, trying to summon mechs—anything to help him.

Suddenly he dropped to the floor, limbs free from the binds. He opened his eyes and witnessed all their torturous mechs explode into dust. Then in a single motion, each bully's nanos flew back into their bodies, knocking them back in the unexpected move.

Jake stormed in, the observant young teen right behind him.

Fully in control of these assholes' nanos, Jake scrambled them inside their bodies, sending them all writhing in pain and collapsing to the floor.

"Doesn't feel so good, does it?"

They couldn't contain their shrieks of agony as their own nanotech attacked them from within.

Artemis struggled to his feet to join Jake.

"You okay?" he asked.

"No, but I think maybe I will be."

Something in his voice worried Jake. There was a melancholy that wasn't there before.

"What should we do about these pricks?"

Artemis looked each one over as they writhed in pain.

"I don't care," he mumbled and walked out of the room.

"Wait! Artemis, don't go."

Jake looked over to the fourteen year old who had come to fetch him.

"You better go too. Thank you for getting me; you did the right thing."

The kid nodded and left.

"Alone at last," Jake said diabolically. "What games shall we play?"

*   *   *

In the morning, when faculty began preparing for their day, Agent Ben Donovan headed to the training room. He was relieved to be off "Sasha babysitting" duty. Conversations with her left a sickening revulsion in his mouth, and he was grateful to not deal with her for a time.

He strode the hall, his mind on lesson plans and what gift to buy mom for her birthday next week.

The training room lights were already on, visible through the seams of the closed double doors.

Cool. Maybe someone already opened the room up, he thought.

Opening the door, he stopped cold. Before him stood a display both shocking and beautiful. Swirls of nanos were formed into a massive, chrome-like statue rising some fifteen feet. Distributed within the folds and curves of the swirling structure were four sobbing teens. They cried out when they caught sight of Ben. Their bodies were contorted within the mech into uncomfortable, unnatural poses, and they were absolutely helpless to free themselves.

Ben ran up to the living statue, panic etched on his face. He had no idea how to help them.

"They deserved it," came a quiet voice near the doorway. Ben spun round to see an exhausted Jake leaning against a wall.

"Release them, Jake," he ordered.

"No problem. I just wanted you to know this was justified."

In an instant the mech liquefied again and the nanos raced back into the teens' bodies. Too weak to move, Rick, Jonas, Mark, and Chloe could only lie on the floor and rub their stiff muscles and wipe tears from their cheeks.

Ben turned to Jake, furious. "Dr. Flint's office. Now!"

CHAPTER 11

"I'm disappointed, Jake," uttered Dr. Flint, leaning forward in his chair and resting his palms on the dark cherrywood desk.

Jake, seated across from him, felt the sting of that statement. He held so much respect for Dr. Flint, letting him down crushed him. Yet, he knew he'd done the right thing. He'd saved Artemis, and he had no regret for his actions. His parents were in the office as well, giving Jake a modicum of relief.

"If you'd seen what they were doing to Artemis," Jake responded. "You would have done the same."

Greg and Tina hung back, but dad couldn't resist giving Jake's shoulder a reassuring squeeze.

"Be that as it may," Dr. Flint began grimly. "I simply cannot have you losing control and abusing those unique gifts of yours. You're liable to incite a full scale panic. If we're lucky, this won't go viral through the complex."

"I'm sorry, Dr. Flint. I reacted to save my friend. I just didn't see any other way to stop them."

Dr. Flint let out a long, exasperated sigh. "I'm afraid I have to agree. This is really my own fault. I should have done this from day one."

Jake and his parents responded with perplexed looks.

"I should have taken you under my wing, so to speak. Sending you in with all the other students was a mistake on my part, and for that I'm sorry. Unique abilities require unique training."

Breathing a collective sigh of relief, the London family relaxed.

"Starting tomorrow, we begin."

"Thank you, Max," said Greg, stepping forward and reaching out to shake the leader's hand.

Dr. Flint hesitated to take his friend's hand, and instead said, "Sorry, Greg. Terrible cold coming on. Wouldn't want to give it to you and force your students to have a substitute."

Greg accepted that and pulled back.

"What about the bullies?" asked Jake.

"They have been dealt with," began Dr. Flint, "and they are no longer students here."

Another sigh of relief. Jake couldn't wait to tell Artemis.

As the Londons rose to leave, Jake paused and turned back to Dr. Flint.

"I need to ask you for a favor," he started nervously.

*　*　*

Trent passed slowly by the corridor to the prison cells, just as he had every day since Sasha's capture. As always, he could see the two guards stationed at desks near the secured door. And, as always, they seemed bored to death.

They sat a good thirty feet from the connecting hallway where Trent now stood. Other students made their way up and down the path, ignoring this all-too-important corridor. The noise was enough to drown out what these two guards spoke about.

He knew they would always be there, and he would never have a legit reason to go beyond those doors. He'd never get his chance to confront, then kill, the murderer of his parents. He had to come to grips with this knowledge, but no matter how hard he tried, he simply could not overcome the desire to choke the life out of Sasha.

The door opened and two guards stepped through, securing it behind them. They began to speak with the seated guards, and, after a moment, they moved on toward the T-connection where Trent stood.

Thinking fast, he leaned against a wall and tried to act casual as the two reached the hallway.

The guards gave him a glance, then moved on to their duties.

Trent turned to leave, and came face to face with Jake. Behind him walked his parents, Bex, and Dr. Flint. *Shit.*

"Trent," smiled Dr. Flint. "Funny we should run into you near the prison."

Trent almost attempted to pass off his proximity to Sasha as a coincidence, but opted for a more direct course. "I want to see her."

They all paused, eyes to their leader. Everyone in this scenario knew the implications of such a request, knew full well Trent's crushing desire for revenge.

Dr. Flint thought for a moment, then shocked everyone with, "I think that is an excellent idea, Trent."

"Wait—what?"

"One look at how she's living will satiate that thirst for vengeance, and you can finally move on with your life."

CHAPTER 12

The observation room glowed under a single overheard light. The rest of
the crew had gone for the evening, and only a single operator sat at the
desk that overlooked Sasha's chamber.

Upon seeing the boss enter with an entourage, the attendant sat up
straight in her chair and struggled to look busy.

"How's our guest this evening?" asked Dr. Flint.

"Cheerful as ever," she quipped, trying to be amusing.

Dr. Flint turned to the others and found them all riveted to the sight
of Sasha in her transparent cage, dim lights lining the surrounding walls.

She sat on her bed, knees up to her chin. Her head was bowed, her
matted hair masking her face.

"Jesus," Trent heard himself mutter.

Jake noted Trent's hand clench to a fist, but his friend kept his cool.

Bex, on the other hand, lost her shit. She backed away from the sight
of Sasha. There she was, right before her, the cause of all her pain and
misery. The catalyst that had murdered hundreds and had caused her to
do the same. Bex had blood on her hands, but it was Sasha who helped put
it there.

She found herself shaking violently, despite her efforts to hide it. All
eyes turned to her. Jake was at her side, arm around her, gently moving her
head to his chest, stroking her hair.

The sobs came next and she was frustrated and embarrassed.

"I'm s-sorry. I didn't expect..."

"It's okay," whispered Jake, "I know."

Greg and Tina also placed consoling hands on Bex's back and shoulder.

Trent couldn't look away from Sasha, hadn't even noticed the commotion.

Dr. Flint stood motionless, observing his daughter's breakdown without so much as a concerned glance. In fact, Jake noted, he almost seemed annoyed by the whole display.

Bex lifted her gaze to meet Jake's. "I'm sorry, Jake. I should have told you how fucked up I am."

"It's on me, Bex. I saw what was happening and didn't do or say anything. I should have been there for you."

"I don't know what's wrong with me. I feel like I'm drowning. I see their faces. I see their bodies."

Jake held her tighter, but locked eyes on Dr. Flint's callous demeanor. *What the hell is wrong with him?*

Trent tore himself from Sasha to see his suffering friend. He started to move toward Bex to comfort her, but then turned back to Sasha. He glanced back to Bex and the others—all eyes were on her breakdown.

At last Dr. Flint moved to his daughter and placed his hands on her shoulders. Jake noted the stiff movement. He clearly had no emotional investment here.

"We're here for you," Dr. Flint began. "I should have seen this coming. I'm sorry I failed you."

Bex could only reply with heaving sobs.

She squeezed Jake's hand as he caressed her back.

The nightmares raced through her mind, a continuous display of blood and suffering. The elite Hunters she'd beheaded in the safe house hallway. The Phalanx agents cut in half before her eyes on the train platform. Sasha's derailment of the train; hundreds of innocent people plummeting to their deaths. Yes, Sasha was to blame for most of the carnage, but Bex couldn't deny the blood on her own hands. She knew her hands were shaking, but was unable to stop them. She was in a tailspin, a downward spiral. Inside she raged, but her countenance displayed only misery.

They all connected in the silence. Surrounded by love, Bex regained her composure. She wiped her tears and hugged each loved one. Taking a deep breath, she sighed heavily, shaking off the last of the episode, though she knew there would be more in her future.

Everyone let out a collective sigh.

Bex looked around the room. "Where's Trent?" she asked.

Dr. Flint spun round and dashed to the one-way mirror, knowing where he'd gone.

*　*　*

Trent pressed his hands against the thick, Plexiglas cell and placed his forehead against the barrier. Three inches separated him from Sasha. His parents' killer. The torturer of his friends. The woman who had tried to kill him and everyone he loved on several occasions. She was so close, and he couldn't touch her.

Sasha sensed someone was near and lifted her head slowly from her tucked up knees. Through strands of matted hair, she squinted to see who had come to visit. Her eyes went wild when she realized Trent stood facing her on the other side of the clear cell wall.

"I know why you're here," she grunted as if even speaking labored her. "Just get it over with."

Trent, forehead and palms still pressed against the clear cage, only sighed. In a hushed whisper, he said, "You deserve it."

She replied in a melancholy tone, "I know."

He wanted nothing more than to lay into her; destroy the obstacle separating them and crush the life from her. Here was his chance, alone with Sasha, exactly the way he'd envisioned his revenge for years. One simple action to start that chain of events.

Liquid metal seeped from his palms, coating the Plexiglas in thin veins of chrome, branching out like tree limbs. All that was needed was his command.

Trent sighed deeply, and recalled his forming mech. He stepped back from the cell, clenching his fists.

"This is not why I'm here. We are running out of time for your Hunters. Have you told us everything? Every hideout and hangout and safe house? I need to know."

Sasha couldn't help notice the urgency in his voice. "I've told you everything. What is it?"

"Someone is killing Mechcrafters out there. And he doesn't discriminate. We know of about a dozen deaths so far."

Sasha rose and staggered toward the clear wall, worry etched upon her face.

"We need to find the rest of the Hunters. Get them off the street," he said.

"Since when do you care about Hunters?" she questioned.

"It's only you I hate. Your faction are just brainwashed victims. I don't hold them accountable. Now tell me where they are holed up."

"There is a place. The last safe house. Please, take me with you. I have to protect them."

"Since when do *you* care about Hunters? Your entire sales pitch is 'we all must die!'"

"I love my children. You don't understand how we believed. You never could. Doesn't matter. My faction is done. But you have to save the rest of them."

"That's the plan. Tell me where."

"Let me come with you."

"You know you're never getting out of that cell, right? Tell me where they are."

Dr. Flint's voice came over the loudspeaker. "That will do, Trent. Come back to the observation deck. Now."

Trent slowly backed toward the door. "We can't save them if you don't tell us."

Sasha turned her gaze from Trent to the giant mirror across the chamber.

"Listen up, Flint. I'm about to blow your mind. You'll never believe where the last safe house is."

* * *

Everyone stood silent, still trying to wrap their minds around the words Sasha had spoken. Trent had rejoined them, and shared their astonished expressions.

"She's got to be full of shit," Trent finally broke the silence.

"She wants her followers rescued. Why would she lie?" offered Greg.

Jake looked at the still-distant Dr. Flint and said, "Your call, Doctor. What do you want to do?"

Dr. Flint turned to the others, all eyes on him.

"What choice do we have? We have to at least check it out."

Trent sighed in concession, "Lions and tigers and bears, oh shit."

CHAPTER 13

Nestled on the eastern side of Griffith Park, at the base of the hill below the famed observatory, stood the LA County Zoo. The high metal posts and gateway conjured images of *Jurassic Park*.

Jake, Trent, Grant, and two Phalanx agents exited their SUV. The parking lot was nearly empty as the zoo had been closed for over an hour.

A rainbow of colored lights danced across the decorative metal animal artwork attached to the fencing. Beyond the gate there was only darkness and the night calls of the zoo's residents.

Jake and Trent kept a secret from Grant. He didn't need to know that Jake was forbidden from field missions. They knew the truth of the matter: he was vital to these excursions.

Jake had lied to his parents, and Bex had backed him, against her better judgment. She understood how important it was that Jake came along on these rescues, even though she detested the idea of him being anywhere near danger.

Grant turned to the Phalanx agents, Leo and Anne. "According to our source, this is the last of the Hunter safe houses. We get this done, and it's mission accomplished."

"Yes sir," they responded in unison.

The five slowly approached the entry area. Trent nudged Jake. "I think I need to call Child Protective Services on your parents."

Jake smiled. *Here it comes.* "And why's that?"

"Letting their little boy go out past his bedtime. Just a shame really."

"Yeah. That's a sad state of affairs. Especially leaving me in the care of a psycho."

Trent sighed. "Damn shame. Gonna have to move you into the system. Another victim of society. I'll come visit, I promise."

"How you going to do that from behind bars?"

The five stopped at the gate.

Grant looked them over. "Alright, even though this is considered a rescue escort, be prepared for resistance. We go in, move straight, and right at the fork toward the tiger compound."

They nodded in agreement.

As one they summoned their liquid nanos from their palms, and used a variety of methods for leaping over the metal fence. Jake stepped on a flat mech disc and floated over. Trent shot one end of a large mech tendril over the fence and used the end closest to him to wrap around his waist and slingshot him over.

The group quietly stalked their way down the main path and veered right at the darkened Treetop Terrace restaurant. They stealthily made their way along the winding path between the Elephants of Asia enclosure and the Amazon Rainforest. They passed the World of Birds Theater, and Grant pointed toward the back fencing against the hillside on the right, just across from the tiger enclosure, grunts and growls from the big cats grabbing everyone's attention.

They spread out along the fence, looking for the clue Sasha had provided. Leo spotted a mark on the hillside about twenty feet up from the fence: a clearing in the brush and a broken tree limb, just as described. Leo waved the others over.

A gleam of bright silver rocketed suddenly from the hillside. A bolt of liquid nanos struck Leo in the chest, sending him up and plummeting into the tiger enclosure.

The others didn't have a moment to react as more mech bolts rained down upon them, each one about a yard in length. Grant, Trent, and Anne summoned mech shields, but Jake focused on the barrage bearing down on them, instantly making the mechs burst into harmless dust.

The disrupted nanos found their way back to their unseen owner, giving away the aggressor's position on the hill. Without a word, Grant, Trent, and Anne launched a barrage of missiles and blades at the source while Jake used his nanos to catapult over the tiger enclosure fence to fetch Leo.

Grant commanded some of his nanos to coat his torso underneath his shirt and propelled himself into the air, soaring toward the enemy. Trent and Anne followed suit. The three gained a better perspective of the terrain and spotted their quarry. A large figure, coated in liquid chrome, made his way through the overgrowth toward the parking lot, and the three gave chase.

In the tiger pit, Jake found Leo on one knee, shaking off the pain from the hard landing. He rushed to his side, immediately scanning the area. Four tigers eyed the strangers from the shadows, some illuminated by the moonlight. Three of the big cats started moving, circling. Their curiosity spurred them on.

"Shit," Leo grunted and stood.

"Time to go," said Jake, and both used their nanos to coat their torsos.

As they rose, one massive tiger leaped and tackled Leo. He screamed as the claws dug into his core.

On the hillside, the coated figure took flight, keeping low among the trees, his pursuers following suit and gaining. Grant conjured and launched a tentacle at their opponent, but it was blocked by the figure's defensive shield launched from his back. Anne sent small, razor sharp blades, several striking home and slicing into the protective nano coating.

The figure countered with his own barrage of blades, striking all three. Trent and Grant took minor hits, but Anne found her throat slashed. She lost focus, accidentally recalling her nanos all at once and crashing hard into the brush.

"Keep on him," ordered Grant and dropped back to aid Anne.

Trent accelerated. *Time to take this bastard down.*

He gained on the enemy, even as he altered course and headed back deeper into the zoo.

Grant found Anne in a heap of tangled branches and foliage, clutching at the gash in her throat. He instantly coated the wound with his nanos, stopping the flow of blood.

In the tiger pit, Jake summoned and sent a large sphere at the attacking beast, knocking it off Leo. Keeping his wits about him, Leo coated his claw wounds with nanos and stood up.

Two more tigers joined the original attacker and stalked their tasty new snacks.

As Jake and Leo coated their torsos and attempted to escape again, all three leaped at them. Leo dodged and rose higher, and Jake conjured a shield that deflected the other two.

They were nearly out of the enclosure when two large mech spikes plunged into them. As they lost focus and dropped back into danger, Jake caught sight of the mech-coated figure racing toward them, Trent not far behind.

They struck the ground hard, and the tigers pounced. Claws dug deep and raked across their torsos, both boys crying out. All four tigers then joined in the feast.

Jake felt his flesh rip across his chest, and he saw a tiger bite down on Leo's neck and jaw, muffling his cries.

The spikes embedded in their bellies dissolved and rejoined their attacker above.

Trent paused and fired an array of small blades, striking the frenzied beasts, buying his friends just enough time to create defenses. Jake and Leo encased their flesh in nanos and willed them to harden. The tigers, only mildly distracted by Trent's attack, returned to their prey to find the tender treats now impossible to rend.

As the boys floated upward, the tigers did their best to pin the morsels to the ground, jumping and swatting at them like birds attempting to flee. Finally, they broke free and rose above to a safe height.

Their enemy took position above the opposite end of the tiger enclosure, facing the three of them. Trent was closest, and he bolted in full force, conjuring two mech pistols in his palms. He fired relentlessly, each mech bullet striking home, but the enemy simply absorbed the hits in his nanotech coating.

The figure sent a long tendril from the coating down into the tiger pit. Suddenly, the tendril went taught and the figure picked up a struggling, flailing tiger and hurled it at Trent. He rolled and flipped his angle to narrowly dodge the living projectile, sending him spinning off course.

Jake, still trying to stop the bleeding from his wounds, sent out his own tendril and caught the poor animal, providing a gentle landing.

Trent lost momentum and came to a hard crash on the asphalt near the enclosure.

Grant came up next to him. "Anne's fine," he uttered, never taking his eyes off the enemy. "Let's take him down."

They charged at the nano-coated foe. Jake and Leo, having patched up their wounds, followed their lead and flew at their target.

The figure, still hovering in the air, launched four tendrils and a barrage of small blades at his attackers. Jake was ready, and used his power to disrupt the weapons and burst them into metallic dust. He tried again, hurling spikes and spears. Jake made quick work of them, filling the air with more dust.

The team neared their target and they all began conjuring weapons. Closing in on him, the enemy seemed calm, serene. As they came upon him, the figure dropped to the ground, landing twenty feet below in the tiger pit's moat, disappearing beneath the surface.

The four charged into the pit, into the moat in pursuit. The tigers gathered and paced at the edge: so many playthings just out of reach.

Searching the depths, the three of them could find no trace of their quarry. He'd escaped them.

Soaring out of the tiger enclosure, they met up with Anne at the entrance to the hidden Hunter base. Her face gave away what they'd find inside; the murderer had already done his handiwork. They entered to perform the grisly task of body count and wound details and the search for any clues.

Over two dozen scared, hiding Hunters had lost their lives in grim, brutal ways.

One question nagged at their thoughts, however. How had the murderer known where to go? He'd been one step ahead of them since the beginning, as if he'd had the same knowledge as they did, but earlier. The conclusion to that train of thought sent panic through them.

Trent called in for the clean-up crew, while Jake pondered how he'd explain to Sasha what had happened to the last of her faction.

*　*　*

Michael Ash arrived after the patrol cars responded to the calls about the chaos at the LA Zoo. A dozen cars, sirens on silent, lined the parking lot, and the entrance had already been barricaded. Flashing his badge, Michael moved through it all with ease.

The destruction near the tiger enclosure was evident: metal fence bent and wrenched, landscape on the hillside torn and broken, and even some of the rock fixtures in the tiger pen showed damage.

The general consensus so far was vandalism, but two eyewitnesses from the Gene Autry Museum across the parking lot told of something else.

From interviewing the witnesses, Michael heard their account of a person in a silver suit—like a haz-mat suit—running through the brush on the hill being chased by others. They also spoke of metallic objects being hurled back and forth at each other. The crime scene investigators didn't place much stock in these details, still leaning toward a case of vandals, but this information struck a chord in Michael. Could this be those same people from the Roxy?

The witnesses had one last detail: five people left the scene in a black SUV.

He would check the footage of the surrounding security cameras, all of which appeared intact.

CHAPTER 14

"The bastard is one of us," Trent grunted to Dr. Flint. Despite their wounds healing, the rescue party looked like hell. Dr. Flint, Greg and Tina, met with the team for their debriefing in Flint's office. He seemed unmoved by the bomb Trent just dropped.

Greg sighed. "I can see no other explanation. How else could the killer have known where this last Hunter safe house was located?"

Tina had not let go of her son since his return to base. He feigned annoyance, but secretly appreciated her smothering. He knew all too well this would not be the end of the conversation. He'd disobeyed his parents and had put himself in danger. Still, he had no regrets. His unique power had saved them during the encounter with the murderer. If he'd played by the rules, some or all of them would be dead.

"We're not done with this, Jake," she ordered. "Life is about to change for you."

"Fair enough," Jake was surprised to hear himself say.

"Let's not be too hasty about this info," Dr. Flint chimed. "We don't want to start a panic. We have to be discreet, otherwise we'll have utter chaos in the halls."

Dismayed by the response, Grant spoke up. "Maybe a little panic is what we need. We are charged with keeping these people protected. We can't leave them unarmed and with no knowledge of the murderer walking among them."

"I'll have security briefed and we'll quietly search the building," offered Dr. Flint.

"I don't understand," added Trent. "Why are you blowing this off?"

"Believe me, I am taking this very seriously. And I'll thank you to trust in my leadership."

Trent's amicable history with the good doctor made him back down. Dr. Flint had taken him under his wing and shown a reckless smart ass how to be a compassionate smart ass. He conceded to Flint's experience and wisdom and sat, though a sense of trepidation consumed him.

"Gauntlet is at your disposal, Doctor. Whatever you need."

"Thank you, Grant. Most appreciated."

Jake looked around the room, and asked, "Who's going to tell Sasha?"

Everyone looked at Jake, and he sighed.

*   *   *

Sasha brought herself out of her stupor. *Had someone approached*?

She fought the urge to scratch her arm. Without her nanos, she didn't heal like she used to, and the flesh had turned raw in the first week of her incarceration. *No scratching. Bide your time. No scratching.*

She quelled the shakes that had begun to plague her since her nanos had been ripped from her. She could hate Jake for doing it. She could hate them all. But she knew, deep down, she deserved this. So she took her punishment day in and day out. *No scratching.*

Movement outside the cell caught her eye. Someone had indeed come in. She looked up to see Jake standing before her on the other side of the Plexiglas.

She rushed to the clear wall, desperate for answers.

"How are they? How many are there? Can I see them?"

Jake sighed. "I'm sorry, Sasha. I'm very, very sorry."

The broken woman before him cracked even further, if that were possible. Her face frozen in a silent scream, her palms pressed against the

Plexiglas, she slid down and collapsed to the floor. At last she found her voice and shrieked a mournful, guttural cry that shook Jake to his core.

In the control room, they all felt her agony in that cry.

Tina fixated on Jake. *Why did we let him do this? Why did he want to?*

Back in the cell room, Jake knelt down to be closer to her. In a forceful whisper, he uttered, "I will find him. And I will make him pay. My way."

She ceased her sobs for a moment, and met his gaze. She murmured back, "Why do you care, after what we did to you?"

"Now that you're here, unable to control them, they were just scared teens, hiding."

More tears filled her eyes. "H-how many?"

"I don't think it's a good idea—"

"Please, Jake. I need to know."

"Twenty eight. We tried. We were too late. I'm really sorry, Sasha."

Sasha became inconsolable. There was nothing more to say. Jake rose, and headed for the exit. She watched him walking away and called out, "I believe you, Jake. I believe you."

In the control room, the adults looked to one another, perplexed.

"Did you get any of that? What did they whisper?" asked Dr. Flint.

Greg and Tina exchanged concerned looks.

* * *

In the cafeteria, Jake's mind drifted and darted with thoughts of the killer. He had to admit, a part of him was relieved his parents had banned him from this investigation. He knew he was out of his league on this now. Still, his gifts made him feel a level of responsibility and duty he couldn't ignore.

Bex noted the distant expression and the untouched lasagna in front of her boyfriend. She gave him a playful nudge.

"Anybody home?" she whispered.

Jake snapped out of it, gave Bex a quick peck on the cheek. "I'm here. Just thinking."

Trent looked up from shoveling pasta into his mouth. "I wish your parents hadn't pulled you out. We need you on this one, Jake."

"You'll be fine. Grant and his team are the best."

Trent chuckled. "Sure, that's why two of them almost died. I mean, you're right. We'll get this done; I just wish we had our wildcard out there to help. But I get it. Your parents are right."

Artemis, still figuring out his place in this new group of friends, observed silently. He felt honored that they had included him, and had even revealed the classified information that the murderer was a Phalanx member in this very building.

"For what it's worth," chimed Artemis, "at least Jake can now be the eyes and ears within these walls, since this is where the killer lives."

Bex gave a cautious look around. "That's what freaks me out the most."

"What's even more bizarre is your dad hasn't sent you away," Jake added. "I wonder why he hasn't sent any of us away? He's okay leaving his daughter exposed to danger?"

"Apply that logic to all of us. Enough of the adults and parents know what's going on, and yet no one has packed up and left," Artemis pointed out.

"A mass exodus would tip off the killer, and we'd never find him then," offered Trent.

"So we are bait for a maniac," quipped Artemis. "How wonderful."

This didn't sit well with Jake. "There's got to be more to this. I'll hit up the parents later."

A commotion of laughter stirred from across the cafeteria. The four friends were shocked to see the expelled bullies eating and having a great time. Rick, Jonas, Mark, and Chloe threw as much food at each other as what reached their mouths. They carried on as if they owned the place.

Trent rose. "Son of a bitch."

Jake did the same. "I don't understand."

"Time to let them know they don't live here anymore," Trent began to move in their direction.

Bex reached across the table and grabbed his sleeve. "No. Don't stir up trouble. Let me talk to dad, see what happened. I'll get to the bottom of this. Just leave it for now."

Accepting her plea, the boys took their seats. "It's a real shit show around here lately," Trent grunted and took a bite of lasagna.

Bex watched the bullies carrying on, and noticed a fifth person approach their table. They were all so happy to see him and showered him with high-fives and fist bumps. Jonas moved his head and revealed the new person to be Dante Barnes.

She froze. Her hands began to shake. She knew he was coming, but nothing could have prepared her for the actual sight of him.

Jake caught her tensing up and followed her gaze to a good looking teen boy among the bullies. He wore his sandy blond hair cropped short and styled, and possessed a chiseled jaw. Jake felt his blood coming to a boil. "That him?"

She nodded, still phased from the sight of her stalker, her ex.

Without a word, Jake rose and stormed toward the asshole table.

Trent took note and followed. "Oh, so we're doing this now? Great."

Jake reached the table and the bullies grew fearful and hushed, looking anywhere in the room except at their nemesis.

Dante held no such fear, looking straight at Jake. "Nice to meet you, Jake." He extended his hand to Jake. "I've heard you can do amazing things."

Jake ignored the offered hand. "I've heard about you too. Stay away from Bex."

"Relax. She and I are ancient history."

"And she wants to keep it that way."

Trent and Artemis had taken supportive stances on either side of Jake. Bex didn't want the situation to explode, and she made her way to them.

"Trust me, Jake. I'm just here to do a job."

Bex put herself between Jake and the still-seated Dante. Ignoring her ex, she looked Jake directly in the eyes. "Come with me. He's not worth it; he's not worth it."

She caressed his cheek and felt his tension dissipate. With that, everyone else relaxed somewhat. Jake sighed and kissed Bex on the forehead, embracing her. As a group, they started back toward their table.

Under his breath, Rick muttered, "He needs his ass kicked."

Dante chuckled. "Go ahead, Rick. There he is."

"Well I mean…. You know…at some point…"

"That's what I thought," finished Dante.

* * *

"We have to tell your father," insisted Jake as he and Bex sat in his room. They had made an attempt to return to a normal life, but homework and sex couldn't hold up against the heady issues of the day.

"There's a lot I need to talk to him about. I don't like that he's not evacuating the students. And why the hell didn't he kick out those jerks like he said?"

"And I don't like that your psycho ex was smiling at us like some used car salesman."

"Look, Jake. You need to keep it together. Dante is not staying forever. As soon as the last of the Hunters are deprogrammed and assimilated, he and his family are gone. Just need to tough it out."

"I don't think I can."

"You have to. Do it for me. Please."

Jake sighed. "Yes. Yes. For you, I'll hold back."

Trent entered the room, saw the lovers seated on the bed. "Sorry, didn't mean to cock block."

Bex laughed. "'No time for love, Doctor Jones.'"

Jake kissed her cheek. "I love it when you do movie quotes, Short Round."

Trent rolled his eyes. "Get a room." He glanced around. "Oh, wait." He took a seat on his own bed, across from the couple.

"So what's the plan now?" asked Jake.

"Refocusing the investigation homeward. Grant is selling an idea to his team to relocate a lot of Gauntlet soldiers here temporarily."

"Think they'll go for it?" asked Bex.

"He's been met with so much opposition over our allegiance.... Tough to say."

"It's been hard, but it's been worth it. I know I've said it before, but you were right to reach out to them. I doubted your vision of an alliance, and I was so wrong."

Trent smiled. "Never gets old hearing Bex Flint say she was wrong."

She threw a pillow at Trent, and the three shared a rare moment of levity.

CHAPTER 15

Deep below the streets in a warehouse district of Los Angeles, The Gauntlet Headquarters buzzed with rumor and gossip among the soldiers as a fateful meeting took place in the War Room.

In the nondescript chamber of flat screens and a large table, Grant MacReady laid out his case to his remaining counsel, Timothy James and Bea Moreno. He knew it would be an uphill battle. Timothy had resisted this alliance since the beginning, but Bea had always seemed open to it. *Would she still, with this new mission?*

"I want to move a company of soldiers into Phalanx."

"What?! Weaken our position here?" Timothy was dumbfounded.

"It's only temporary. The killer is among them. Phalanx needs all the help we can offer to flush him out and end this."

Timothy scoffed. "End what? No Gauntlet soldiers have been lost to this murderer. As far as I'm concerned this is a Phalanx issue."

"You still don't get it," Grant gritted his teeth. "We all rise together. The days of war are over."

"And look what's happened since? Gauntlet is the lap dog of the government once again, and we handed over the greatest weapon in Mechcraft history to our oppressors."

Grant looked to Bea for support. "Can you please talk some sense into him?"

Bea sat up straighter, looked to both men, and rested her eyes on Grant. "I've been with you on this since the beginning. But we took heavy losses on Disruption Day, and since then it seems as though chaos has filled their house. Why should we sacrifice any more for them? No, I have to agree with Timothy. Let Phalanx sort this out."

"I can't believe what I'm hearing. Since when do we turn our backs on those in need? Since when do we abandon our people?"

"Phalanx is not our people," grunted Timothy.

"That's your final decision, then?"

His counsel both nodded.

"Very well. As Gauntlet leader, I'm ordering a company of soldiers to temporarily reside and assist Phalanx in the investigation for the killer. I'm going to bring us into the future, even if I have to drag you two kicking and screaming."

"Bea and I thought it might come to this. We agree to a position of No Confidence in the current leadership of Gauntlet, and are placing you under arrest."

"What?! That is insane. I'm not going anywhere. The soldiers will support me. They'll never stand for this."

"I beg to differ," replied Timothy and nodded to Bea.

Bea rose and opened the door. Five soldiers entered, looking to Timothy.

"I'm sorry, Grant. You were a fine leader until this Phalanx business. Now, you leave us no choice." He nodded at the soldiers.

The three men and two women spread out behind Grant. One of the women gave the command, "Come with us, sir."

Grant saw no other option, no other way out. With deep regret, he resisted. He immediately launched a burst of liquid metal from his hands and neck, blasting out in a large radius around him and pummeling the soldiers, Timothy, and Bea. The soldiers stumbled back, caught off guard, giving Grant the moment he needed. He bolted out the door.

Running the corridor, he reached the large vehicle bay just as the alarm sounded. His soldiers looked at their fleeing leader in utter confusion, but Bea's voice boomed over the loudspeaker, and the chase was on.

Soldiers fired spheres and shields to impede Grant, but not harm him. He ducked and dodged, but kept his momentum. He retaliated with a widespread shield behind him that obscured their view, giving him some distance.

Grabbing an SUV, he drove hard and fast for the exit ramp. The sensors detected a vehicle approaching and lowered the ramp automatically. In seconds, he would be free and clear.

Just as he was about to reach the ramp, the override kicked in, pressed by Bea or Timothy no doubt, and the ramp began to rise. He slammed on the gas, determined to make it. The front wheels crossed onto the lifting ramp, but at mid-body, the edge of the rising ramp scraped the underside and lifted the SUV off the ground—stopping Grant cold.

The ramp jammed and ground into the top and bottom of the SUV as it attempted to close all the way. The integrity began to give, and Grant scrambled out. He still had an edge, was still far ahead of his pursuers. He ran the rest of the way up the ramp to the ground level inside the empty warehouse that disguised the base entrance.

He reached the exit and ran headlong into the nearly-deserted industrial streets, the afternoon sun giving him no shadows in which to hide. The buildings seemed to close in on him as he ran on and on. Betrayed and backstabbed by his own, Grant knew there was but one place for him. He would regroup at Phalanx, and there he'd plot and plan how to regain his role in Gauntlet. *Surely, they all didn't agree with the traitors.*

He was blocks away by the time the ramp was lowered once again and the damaged vehicle moved aside. Still, Grant heard them coming. He needed to get out of sight.

Four SUVs and six motorcycles raced in different directions to spot and capture their fugitive leader. They passed by him without ever spotting their quarry.

When the coast was clear, a metallic utility box, commonly seen next to most buildings, melted away, revealing Grant inside. He reabsorbed his nanos and pressed on. He had miles to go. He called the one person he could still trust.

CHAPTER 16

Dante Barnes hated being back in Los Angeles, but orders were orders. His parents had no clue why he'd been so against the trip. They had no idea how Bex had humiliated him in that alley two years ago. *How could she do that to him?*

The plan was always Dante and Bex, together forever. Marriage. Kids. The whole thing. They were going to be the power couple one day. He'd had it all worked out. *Why couldn't she see it? Why did she fuck it all up?*

Returning to this god-awful place presented a choice for him. Either exact punishing revenge upon her, or try to win her back. He was still on the fence; it could go either way.

Then there was Jake. This freak. *He gets to be with Bex? I don't think so.* He would expose this clown, show them all what Jake truly was: unstable and untrustworthy. He'd heard all the stories, all the accounts. He wasn't buying into Jake's show of loyalty and compassion. No way.

Dante stood outside his dorm room, at the rail three stories up, looking out over the main hall. The mech piping, in all its colors and movement, was always impressive. He watched the students in the center practicing their Mechcraft. Some mock battled. Others practiced intricate patterns and designs. And a few took to the air, flying and darting under mech power.

He had once loved this place. Bex had taken that away from him.

Time to get to work. Deprogramming these Hunter scumbags was not a task he relished, but orders are orders. The price of being good at one's job.

As he walked the hall toward the elevator, a poster caught his eye. A spring dance. It always amused him how Dr. Flint tried so hard to bring normalcy to the Mechcrafters. Dances and classes. A valiant effort, but a waste of time. These teens were destined for greatness. There was nothing normal about them, nor the lives they would lead. That's okay. *Let us all play our part.*

* * *

Bex sat across from her father in his office. Again, something was off about him. *Was his illness returning? No, he no longer needed the cane, and he didn't seem weak at all. What was this coldness all about?*

"Bex, it's a terrible idea to evacuate these families. Last thing we want is to tip off this killer that we're on to him. I don't like leaving people vulnerable any more than you do, and I hope to have this wrapped up in a matter of days. I have all the best working on it."

"But dad, the danger this puts them in."

"I have weighed the risks, and I am comfortable with the numbers."

"This isn't like you. Since when are you willing to trade lives away?"

"I'm sorry you feel this way, daughter. But you're going to just have to trust me."

"Does this have anything to do with Project Ares?" she prodded.

"Ares?" he asked.

"Stop. I already saw references to it. You don't have to lie to me."

"Very well. No, these events have nothing to do with the classified project your prying eyes came across. Ares is none of your business, and I'll thank you to leave it be."

"Fine. Okay. And what about the bullies? You told us they would be expelled."

"I spoke too soon, I'm afraid. I had a long talk with their parents, and they have assured me they will take care of their children's behavior patterns. I have assurances this won't happen again."

"So just like that, they get away with torturing Artemis?"

"No. They are being disciplined. Extra work details. Detention for a month."

Bex's frustration grew into rage. She was so taken aback by her father's attitude, she found herself speechless.

"If there is nothing else, I have a lot of work to do."

She fought back tears and rose. She wanted to say something, do something to shake him from this funk. Dejected, she merely left.

*　*　*

Bex arrived at the deprogramming session to find Dante and his parents, Paul and Karen, already there. They listened to the other adult staff and Neera update them on what had been been done so far and what was still needed.

Bex took a deep breath, steeled herself, and joined the huddle. Dante barely acknowledged her, keeping it all professional, and she was relieved.

Guards escorted the first group of the day in: thirty nervous and frustrated Hunters.

CHAPTER 17

Trent entered Dr. Flint's office, trepidation filling him. Flint must know something. He stood in the doorway, and Flint motioned for him to sit. He was wrapping up a phone call.

"Yes, I understand. And if we hear of anything, we'll let you know. Very well. Goodbye."

Trent sat and waited. Dr. Flint looked him over.

"That was a Mr. James from Gauntlet."

"Oh?"

"It seems Grant MacReady has gone missing. You wouldn't happen to know anything about that, would you?"

"Missing? No. Nothing at all."

"Please do keep an eye out. They sound very desperate to have him back. You sure you haven't spoken to him or seen him?"

"No, sir. Not in a couple days."

"Very well. That's all."

"Okay."

Trent headed for the door, relieved to not have been pressed on the issue.

Dr. Flint had one more thing to add. "Oh, and Trent."

"Yes?"

"When you leave, please have Grant meet me in my office as soon as possible."

He sighed. The jig had been up all along. "Will do, doc."

*   *   *

In minutes, the ousted leader of Gauntlet found himself sitting with Dr. Flint.

"This puts me in an awkward position, Grant."

"I know, and I apologize. I really had no other option."

"Agreed. But now what to do with you? Clearly we can't hand you over to Gauntlet, and I doubt you'd let us take that path anyway."

"I'd like to make myself useful here, if that's alright."

"I'm sure we can find something to keep you busy. Welcome to Phalanx."

Grant moved to shake hands, but Flint didn't offer his in return.

"Sorry, I've got a cold. Wouldn't want to get you sick."

A cold? Mechcrafters don't get sick. What's up with Flint? Maybe Bex is right to be suspicious of his behavior.

"Very true, Max. Thanks again for letting me stay."

*   *   *

At dinner, Trent, Jake, Bex, and Artemis enjoyed an uneventful meal in the cafeteria. The bullies behaved themselves. Dante stayed quiet for the most part. Grant dined with the staff and appeared to be fitting right in.

Trent turned to Artemis. "How about a practice session after dinner?"

He felt terrible for what the kid had gone through after their last session. He hoped training him up more would boost his confidence.

"I don't think so."

"Come on, Arty. Don't give up on this just yet. I have some cool things to show you."

"I'm a hopeless case, I'm afraid."

"Bullshit," retorted Trent. "You are right on the verge of getting this. You're so close now. I won't let you give up, my young Padawan."

"He's right. Plus there's no winning an argument with Trent," added Bex.

"My advice," began Jake, "save yourself the headache and just let Trent have his way."

Artemis sighed. "No use arguing those valid points."

"You won't be sorry," finished Trent.

"Meanwhile," began Jake, "it's a good time to investigate our killer."

"Count me in," added Bex confidently.

"You're sure?"

"Yes. It's time to get back in the game. Long past time."

Jake looked at her proudly. Her strength and courage never ceased to amaze him.

She noted his surprised visage. "What?" she smiled. "I had a breakthrough the other day. I'm scared and nervous, but ready to be a part of this again. Besides, you two clowns definitely need my help."

* * *

Later, Trent led Artemis into the gym. Artemis took deep breaths to quell his anxiety over what had happened last time he practiced in this room. His trepidation washed away when he spotted who waited for them.

Grant MacReady stood tall and straight in full Gauntlet camouflage uniform in the center of the gym, ready for his role as teacher.

"Artemis, I give you the leader of Gauntlet and hero of Disruption Day, Grant MacReady."

Grant stepped forward and shook Artemis' hand.

"No introduction needed," quipped Artemis. "You, sir, are a legend!"

"I don't know about all that, Artemis," he replied humbly. "But it is a pleasure to meet you."

"You as well, sir!"

"Call me Grant."

"Yes, sir, Grant, sir!"

Trent started toward the door. "I'll leave you to it, then."

Incredulous, Artemis turned to Grant. "*You're* going to train me?"

"If you'll have me."

* * *

Trent caught up with Bex and Jake at the prison entrance. The posted guards, used to seeing Bex come and go, granted them entry without question. Walking briskly past the cells, Jake noted a decrease in the number of Hunters: deprogramming success evident.

In the control room overlooking Sasha's cell, they set to work inspecting desks, corners, lights. They sought any sort of listening device. They deduced someone had listened in on the conversation when Sasha had revealed the LA Zoo safe house. The interloper had heard all the locations, in fact. No other way he could have beaten the rescue team to each site.

As always, Ben Donovan manned his post. Bored with no further line of questioning, he simply read the latest Palahniuk novel, ignoring the teens and their din.

Meeting in the middle of the room, the exasperated trio conceded the room was void of any sinister devices.

"What now?" asked Bex.

"It has to be here. How else?" sighed Jake.

"There is one other possibility," added Trent.

"One of us tipped off the killer," said Bex.

"Or *is* the killer," concluded Trent.

Jake scoffed. "Ridiculous. Who was there? The three of us, Dr. Flint, my parents, and the staff."

"If they aren't the killer, they could have been wearing a wire," chimed Ben Donovan, peeking up from his book.

The three turned to him.

"That is, if one of us isn't the actual killer."

"You really think that's a possibility?" asked Trent.

"Makes the most sense, doesn't it?"

*   *   *

The hour was late, but Dante couldn't sleep. The emptiness of his temporary housing annoyed him. For his short stay, he was given an empty dorm room, while his parents stayed in one of the staff apartments.

He was relieved he had no roommate to deal with, but the blank walls and silence seemed to be keeping him awake. Truth was, he couldn't get Bex out of his mind.

Do I kill her or kiss her? Both sound like a solid plan.

Giving up on getting any sleep, Dante dressed and left his room.

He wandered the quiet hall of the Phalanx headquarters, overlooking the large practice arena and all its mech glory. As he approached the elevators, a door opening across the empty chasm caught his attention. One story down, he saw Bex step out of Jake's room, and turn to face him in the doorway.

Dante paused to watch them. As they kissed, Bex's hand caressed Jake's cheek, and he pulled her tight to him. Dante felt sick. This vision stung him to his core. Their passion resurrected his own for her, and memories of their intimacy flooded his mind. They were each other's first, and it was special. He still recalled the curves of her body, the taste of her lips, the smell of her hair.

I can't believe she's with him. How can she love a freak like that?

At last they parted, and Bex headed down the hall, blowing Jake a final kiss as he closed his door. She was alone.

Before he knew it, he had changed direction. He took the stairs down to Bex's floor, and made his way swiftly toward her. He did his best to remain undetected. The plan was to "accidentally" run into her and strike up a casual conversation, with the goal of getting her to feel safe around him. He wanted to gain her trust back. Beyond that, he really didn't know which way he'd go; that would depend largely upon her reactions.

As he drew closer, he had to resist the urge to throw out the plan and simply launch mechs at her back and end this all right now.

"Oh hey, Bex," he called. "I thought that was you."

Bex turned and stifled a cringe at the sight of Dante approaching.

"Couldn't sleep either?"

"What do you want, Dante?" she asked coldly.

"Nothing at all," he began. "Just saw you and thought I'd say hello. Look, I know we ended badly. Really badly. But I want you to know that, for me, it's all in the past. Now I just want to help these kids find their way out of the brainwashing."

"I'm glad you feel that way," she managed to say, her walls still up.

"I think you and Neera are doing an excellent job."

"Thanks."

Feeling he'd made as much progress as possible, he turned to leave. "See you tomorrow."

She sighed, and called to him, "Dante, wait."

He paused, smiling. "Yeah?"

"I need to tell you I am really sorry for what happened. I should never have attacked you. Regardless of our issues, it was wrong of me to lash out like that, and I'm so sorry."

Dante was taken aback. He was so caught off guard by her apology, he didn't know what to say.

Bex continued, "I think I can be a big help with the deprogramming. I'm sure you and your parents being here will speed up our progress a lot."

He finally found his voice. "Thanks for saying all that. I...didn't expect it. And I am very happy to be part of this team. We'll help out and get this done, then head back to DC."

"It's good to have this closure," she added.

"I think so too. Well, I guess I'll see you tomorrow." He waved as he casually strode back down the hall.

Bex let out a sigh of relief. Part of her expected all-out revenge from him. His humility threw her, but she knew better than to believe it. No, Dante Barnes was not the type to change.

CHAPTER 18

The lesson with Grant taught Artemis more than he could have anticipated. The Gauntlet leader had helped him summon and actually hold the shape of a mech, allowing him to mentally maneuver it around the room.

Feeling overjoyed with a dose of confidence thrown in, Artemis strode the hall with his head up, the first time in a long time. He couldn't wait to tell dad.

He was well on his way to being a true Mechcrafter. Maybe one day he could even go on missions with Jake, Bex, and Trent. He truly admired them, and couldn't believe they were his friends.

And maybe the days of being bullied were finally behind him.

As if on cue, the asshole crew came into view. Chloe, Jonas, Mark, Rick, and Dante walked briskly across his path on an intersecting corridor. Artemis froze. He looked left and right—nowhere to hide. Thankfully, the motley group paid him no mind and kept going, evidently with somewhere to be. In moments they were out of his sight.

He crept to the corner and dared to peer around it. They seemed so determined in their stride. *What were they up to?*

Against his better judgment, Artemis followed them at a respectable distance. He knew this was complete folly, and if these hooligans discovered his clandestine pursuit, he'd surely end up in the hospital—or worse. But the desire to prove his worth to his friends drew him further on.

The group made their way through the rec area, the open air common area, and into the staff halls. This time of day, much of the faculty was in the cafeteria or handling after class meetings. These corridors were empty. Students were clearly restricted from this part of the building, yet here they were.

They turned a few corners and stopped at a door. From his vantage, Artemis couldn't make out what the title above the door read. Chloe summoned a thin mech and tripped the lock. They entered and closed the door behind them.

Artemis made his way and discovered the door gave access to the Faculty Training Facility. He'd never been here, nor should he ever have cause to be. He listened at the door; only silence on the other side. With a deep sigh, Artemis opened the door and entered the dark room.

He was in an office or reception area. As his eyes adjusted, he made out a desk, chair, file cabinet situation to his right. Directly in front was another door. To his left, a built-in rack was piled with towels and another stored water bottles. *Why go here of all places?*

He stepped quietly forward. He had to get the intel on them, had to show his friends he deserved to be part of their group. Another step. Another. The door was almost within reach.

A metallic scraping noise from above froze him where he stood. The blow struck him in the back of the head before he had time to gaze up at his attacker, and his vision turned to black.

*   *   *

Dr. Flint requesting to meet with Jake at such a late hour struck him as odd, but he figured the boss's schedule only allowed for this strange time. And instead of meeting in the training room, or even the open practice area in the center, the two met in Dr. Flint's office.

"No need for large spaces. You already know how to conjure. Our purpose here is more...philosophical, as it were," Dr. Flint stated.

"Thanks for this, doctor."

"I was a fool to have you in with the other students and staff on day one. Your unique gifts cause unease in the ranks."

"That's putting it mildly."

"So if they see that you have full control over your abilities, hopefully they will come to accept you."

"At this point, I'll do whatever it takes."

"Excellent. Let's begin."

Over the course of an hour, Dr. Flint gave lessons in control of conjured mechs, having Jake strive for accuracy and form in his creations and actions. The mechs were made to move in specific patterns and designs that became mentally exhausting for Jake.

All the while, Dr. Flint spoke in a steady stream of dialogue to lift his spirits and drive home the lessons of control.

"In the end, our nanotech is an extension of ourselves. A symbiotic relationship of host and companion. They are you; you are them."

* * *

By midnight, Phalanx had calmed to a tranquil silence. Students, faculty, and most of security had all gone to bed. The nightshift guards fulfilled their patrols and stood their posts in quiet concentration.

In Trent and Jake's room, the two slept hard, the day's activities taking their toll. Jake's phone ringing broke the silence, jarring him awake.

He answered, and before he could utter any words, Sophie's panicked voice cut in. She whispered urgently, "Jake! Jake! He's here. Can you hear me?"

Jake, barely awake, tried to focus. "Wh-what? Who is—"

"At the underground. Oh my god, *he's killing everyone*. Help us!"

The phone cut out, silence once again.

In less than a minute, Trent and Jake were racing from Phalanx toward the underground fight arena. The guards had tried to stop them, ignoring their urgent pleas to sound the alarm and rally the troops, but Trent gunned the car and smashed through the gate.

"Shouldn't we grab Grant?" posed Jake.

"Call him. Call everyone!" yelled Trent.

* * *

The warehouse was bathed in darkness. Jake and Trent parked and entered through the large main door, which had been viciously torn from its sliding track. Inside, all but two of the overhead fluorescent lights had been destroyed. The remaining two provided only the dimmest of light, in a perfect horror film slow strobe effect. The cage arena was wrenched and twisted. The bar lay broken and toppled. Bodies lay strewn about the place. Fatal wounds revealed themselves on some, while others lay twisted and contorted in inhuman ways.

Overwhelmed by the madness before them, the two staggered their way in deeper.

Commotion in the far corner snapped them to attention. Metal twisting and wood splintering echoed off the warehouse walls. A scream sent them running around the crumbled bar.

Into their view came the chrome-coated Mechcrafter, massive and imposing. Facing off against him were Sophie and two young teens, boys, no older than fifteen. They fought against their attacker with courage and voracity, working as a team to launch multiple attacks of spikes and blades at the enemy. When the murderer struck back, they pooled their powers to create tough shields that blocked the tendrils thrown at them.

Trent wasted no time, summoning and launching several, foot-long blades as he raced toward the killer.

Seeing the new threat, the Mechcrafter summoned a shield against the incoming blades.

Jake countered by disrupting the shield, blasting it to dust. Trent's weapons sliced through the killer's mech armor, digging deep. The killer fought on, unaffected by Trent's strike.

No time to ponder this shocking development, Trent reached the young Mechcrafters and recalled his nanos to form shields with them. Jake held his ground on the periphery, and disrupted the killer's attacks as fast as his abilities would allow. This bastard was quick—really quick.

The chrome killer launched blades, tentacles, battering rams, all in an attempt to breach his victims' defenses. The teens retaliated in kind, but the killer's armor continually morphed to repel each attack. Even Jake's powers could not sway the battle.

A stalemate solidified. Trent wasn't sure how long they could keep this up. He could see the stamina of these teens diminishing. Sooner or later their defenses would fail.

Jake noted the situation as well and took action. Changing tactics, he seized control of the nanos encasing the killer and forced them to lift their owner fast into the air, slamming him into the metal warehouse ceiling.

"Run!" shouted Trent to spur them on. He led the teens past Jake and toward the exit.

The killer, even pinned to the ceiling, was not finished. He fired metallic bolts at Jake and the fleeing teens. Jake was able to disrupt the bolts aimed at the teens, but took the hit from the one meant for him. The strike knocked him back, forcing him to mentally release his hold on the killer, who levitated himself immediately toward the teens.

Trent rushed them through the exit just as a barrage of deadly blades peppered the metal door. The killer landed and blasted through the already mangled warehouse exit, and was met in the parking lot by dozens of Phalanx Mechcrafters.

Trent and the teens disappeared behind the frontline of battle ready agents, Grant, Greg, and Tina standing in the lead. The killer halted his momentum, assessing his odds against nearly one hundred opponents.

Jake staggered to the door and blasted the armor with his disruptive power. The nanotech armor on the killer began to dissolve, turning the mech to nano dust. He turned on Jake, but the simultaneous attack from the small army blasted him. All manner of mechs sliced, stabbed, pummeled, and pinned the murderer to the ground.

Jake circled around to join his people and stay out of the line of fire. He then joined their attack by disrupting the mech armor once again, hoping to expose weaknesses and reveal the identity of this brutal killer.

The murderer became completely immobilized as assault after assault pounded him. But Jake noticed something wrong. His disruption was going deep now, dissolving more and more nanos, and yet no flesh was exposed. By this time, he should have at least seen a hand or part of this guy's head. So far, nothing but nanos.

Suddenly, the pinned figure melted completely into a pool of inanimate liquid chrome on the asphalt. The Phalanx agents halted their attack to assess what had happened. They looked around in trepidation, Grant easing forward, nanos levitating above his palms, ready to strike.

"What's going on, Jake?" asked Grant.

"I don't know."

"Where's the body?"

Trent recalled Sasha's trickery in the basement of her mansion not so long ago. "Could have been a mimic."

Grant, Jake, and Trent reached the pooled nanos.

"A mimic can launch attacks like that?" asked Grant.

"No idea. This is new."

The nanos slowly floated away in the breeze, lifeless, harmless.

"Then we still have a murderer out there."

The Mechcrafters approached and began several discussions on next steps and what this turn of events could mean. Only Jake watched the nanos take to the wind. There was something not right here something they were all missing.

Sophie ran up to Jake and hugged him. "I knew I made the right call."

"That's twice you've lived to tell the tale."

"Don't remind me."

Jake caught a glimpse of the nanos gathering together in the distance. *Were they reforming? Or swirling randomly in the breeze?*

A second later, the nanos were beyond sight.

"I think you better come to Phalanx for now."

"No argument from me this time."

They rejoined the group; some were already using their craft to repair the warehouse, others had ventured inside to assist with the dead.

Tina hugged her son then scolded him. "It seems as though we have no authority at all anymore."

"Sorry, Mom. I had no choice."

"I know. You did the right thing. I just hate that you had to."

A few Mechcrafters staggered out of the warehouse, visibly shaken. A few vomited.

Greg put a reassuring arm around Jake's shoulder. His son had already seen too much. He feared what all this violence and horror was doing to him.

"How many are in there?" he asked cautiously.

"Too many. More than we've seen before."

"I'd estimate over fifty dead," added Trent, seemingly unaffected by the tragic loss.

Greg put his other arm around Tina.

"We never anticipated this. Never could have imagined this would be your life, Jake."

"Doesn't matter. Here we are, and we have to deal with what's coming."

CHAPTER 19

After hours taking care of the warehouse arena location, the Mechcrafters finally returned home to Phalanx just as dawn approached.

In the foyer, Bex loomed in the shadow cast by dawn's light. Upon seeing Jake, she rushed to hug him tight. Not wanting to let him go, she only did when Trent came into view. She embraced him next, then slugged his arm.

"You both could have been killed!"

Trent smiled at Jake. "A real hero's welcome."

Sophie and the two other survivors walked in, exhausted. Doctors escorted them to the medical ward. Bex sighed. "You guys did good."

"Not good enough. The death toll—"

"I heard."

They fell silent, no one knew what to say in the face of such tragedy.

Bex sighed. "There's more. Artemis was found unconscious in the staff area."

"Jesus. Is he alright?" urged Jake.

"What happened?" prodded Trent.

"We don't know; he's still out. Let's go see him."

*　*　*

Artemis lay unconscious in the hospital bed, IV and monitors around him. His Mechcraft had healed his body, but the brain was a whole different animal.

The friends stood over him, expressions of concern on their faces. "His dad was already here; he is considering pulling Artemis out of the program, but wants to hear what his son has to say when he wakes up," Bex said.

"And he was found in the staff area? What was he doing there?" pondered Trent.

"Doctors say he should come around soon. He's got a concussion from the injury, but there should be no permanent damage," replied Bex.

"We'll get our answers then. Someone did this to him, and I'm going to make them pay."

Jake added, "*We* are going to make them pay."

Bex began to pace at the foot of the bed. She pulled out a raspberry-scented hand sanitizer and gave her palm a generous portion.

Jake noted her nervousness and knew her anxiety was rising once again.

"What is happening here?" she began. "There's nowhere safe anymore. We are all vulnerable."

Trent's anger calmed. "Don't worry, Bex. We'll protect you."

Jake took her hand, reassuringly. "I won't leave your side."

"I'm not some delicate flower. I can handle shit. But these things happening...we can't protect anybody. Our heroics just won't be enough."

* * *

Dr. Flint gazed across his desk at the gathered staff. Greg and Tina London and four others argued their case to their boss.

"Max, I don't see how we can do this and still keep everyone safe," pleaded Greg.

"Why are you pushing this?" Tina asked.

"Things being what they are, it is imperative we show these kids a sense of normalcy. Their mental wellbeing depends on stability. The dance will proceed as planned."

Greg could barely control his anger. "It's too risky. What's wrong with you?"

"Disagree with me all you like. The festivities will go on. We'll add security; we'll take precautions, but these teens will have their time. Now, if there's nothing else? I have a faction to run, and apparently we still have a murderer on the loose, according to your report."

* * *

This disconnect from their old friend permeated their every thought as they walked back to their apartment. Dr. Flint's behavior had become increasingly strange: cold, distant, almost irrational.

But this latest shift sent Greg from concern to rage.

"What can we do?" Tina asked him as he paced the floor.

"Let's gather the staff. We aren't going to let Flint play this game."

"Are you talking about a coup?"

"No, that would not end well for any of us. We'll let Flint think we're on board, but we'll have our own tactics in place at the dance."

"I can't believe we're having this conversation," sighed Tina.

"I can't believe Flint is putting us in a position to have to."

CHAPTER 20

Over the next few days, preparations for the dance ramped up as dozens of kids jumped in to help. Everything from making traditional posters and banners, to creating elaborate mech streamers and dancing dragons, generated a wondrous, fantasy ambiance in the main open chamber.

Fears of the murderer were quelled by the efforts of the staff to downplay the danger, as well as the pure resilience of the teens to compartmentalize life's tragedies and triumphs. Assurances of extra guards, curfews, and the buddy system allowed the students to focus on just being kids.

Trent worked closely with Grant on plans to recon all the known Mechcrafter hang outs, canvasing Los Angeles in an effort to find and rescue any factionless stragglers.

Bex worked with Neera and Dante on deprogramming Hunters. She despised spending time with her ex, but had to concede that having the extra staff was streamlining their efforts to aid and reintroduce the former enemies to the concept of free will.

Jake continued his private lessons with Dr. Flint, away from his peers. All the adults in his life told him this was best: to hide his abilities, to mask his true self. This isolation frustrated him to no end. He still saw his friends at mealtime and after hours, but it just wasn't the same. He began to doubt the benefits of isolation, feeling progressively stronger that he should be in with all the student body so they could get used to him and overcome their fears.

Sophie clung to Jake's side whenever he was out in the common areas. If he was outside his room and finished with Dr. Flint's training, she was with him. Despite her prowess in the fighting arena, the young girl felt terrified for the first time in her life. Having witnessed and survived the murderer twice, her fear was palpable.

Jake understood, and therefore tolerated having a shadow for the time being. Taking up his bedside vigil next to Artemis once again, Sophie joined him, plopping herself on the chair next to him. She had adorned herself with spiraling nanos around her trademark pigtails that hung down past her shoulders. A swirling mech bracelet gleamed from each wrist. The kid was sharp with the details.

"Why won't he wake up?" she asked, breaking the silence.

"I don't know. I thought having Mechcraft meant this kind of thing couldn't happen."

She slowly reached out her hand, trying to be sly, and nudged Artemis' arm. He did not stir. Jake gave her a stern look that melted into a smile.

"Nice try, Sophie."

"At this point, I'm willing to try anything. I get that he has all this info and stuff, but man, this is boring."

"You could go to the gym, get some practice. Or the game room, meet some of the students."

"Nah, I'm good right here."

"Sophie, just because they belong to a faction doesn't make them bad, or sheep, or assholes."

"Maybe. Maybe not."

"Well, if you're going to make a home here, you'll need to make friends at some point."

"Home? Oh hell no. This is just a stopover till the coast is clear from the psycho on the loose. You couldn't pay me to stick around here permanent-like."

"That's too bad. I was hoping you'd stay and teach me how to fight."

"Very funny," she quipped and slugged his arm.

Regardless of her protestations, Sophie couldn't deny her longing to stay in a safe place, off the streets. It had been so long since she'd felt genuinely at home. Of course she'd never admit that to Jake or anyone else.

* * *

Dante played his game to perfection. After just a couple weeks of good behavior in front of Bex, she had already dropped her guard somewhat around him. He had a mountain of ground to make up if he was to win her back. He'd overplayed his hand two years ago, and would not make that mistake again. This time he'd keep himself in check until she was under his control. Then he could be himself, and she'd have to accept him. It only made sense for their union: the most powerful family in Washington DC and the most powerful family in Los Angeles. She had to see the logic. If not, well then, in time, he'd show her his vision of their future.

First things first: get rid of Jake.

Sitting in the cafeteria with Bex and Neera, Dante put on a smile even as he schemed. Their work for the day was finished, with several emotional breakthroughs among the former Hunters. They celebrated the victory.

The adults finally left, and it was just the three of them.

"Even with the new entries the boys keep finding, we're nearly finished with the deprogramming," Bex declared. "And most have already acclimated to Phalanx culture."

"Then what ever will we do with our time?" laughed Neera.

Bex stared at Dante. "I'm sure you'll be heading back to DC."

"Not so sure," he began with a smile. "Mom and Dad are taking a liking to the LA headquarters. I wouldn't be surprised at all if we stayed."

Bex frowned. *Dear god, no.*

"I'm going to ask Dr. Flint to be assigned to field work," piped in Neera. "I've wanted to see what it is you do out there, Bex. Seems quite the adventure."

Bex sighed. She used to see things that way. "It's not always what it's cracked up to be. For me, I'll take a nice comfy desk job for a while."

Dante laughed. "Do we even have such a thing?"

"Teaching, then. Something quiet for a change."

"That does not sound like the Bex I know," Dante teased.

"That's because you don't know me at all."

CHAPTER 21

"So the great Jake London has been grounded," Sasha declared and cracked a thin smile, the first Jake had seen since she held dominion over him at the Hunter HQ those months ago. "They don't realize what you are, Jake. They don't understand at all. You should be out there on the front line, taking on this bastard. Not hiding away here. Oh, Tina..." she trailed off shaking her head.

Jake had paid Sasha a late night visit. Dr. Flint had granted Jake unhindered access to their most prized captive with the condition that any session would be recorded for analysis.

At first Jake didn't know why he felt compelled to see his would-be killer, but eventually decided it was their mutual uniqueness that drew him to her. She was a vile pariah, one of a kind in her thoughts and deeds, but Jake, too, was a singularity, often shunned for simply being who he was born to be. Jake sincerely believed Sasha understood him in a way no one else could. As demented as that sounded, he nevertheless pursued these after hours calls.

"I think they've gathered most every Hunter and factionless Mechcrafter now. At least there's that."

"But no clues on the mass murderer, I assume?"

"I'm not allowed to say."

"Of course. Forget I asked. So what now?"

"Keep up the hunt, I guess."

"No, I mean, what are you doing here tonight?"

"I don't really know."

"I'll tell you. I'm the only one who you know truly understands you. They're holding you back, Jake."

"Who?"

"All of them. Deep down, even the ones who love you also fear you. They think that by controlling you, they protect you—and themselves."

"You got it all wrong."

"Oh no, it's nothing on the surface. This fear is buried deep. So deep, none of them would even know it's there. Think about it. What have they done ever since you reached the safety of this place?"

"I don't know. Train me?"

"Sure, train you in their old Mechcraft ways. No, Jake. What they're doing is keeping you from your potential, attempting to control you. Tina. Greg. Trent. Even Bex. They love you, but they're afraid."

"I don't believe you."

"Fine. Don't," she shrugged. "Just think about it the next field mission you go on. Oh wait; you're banned from those now."

Jake shifted in his chair. "Stop trying to get in my head."

"You know I'm telling the truth."

*　*　*

Silently observing the conversation from the control room, agent Ben Donovan seethed. For months he'd had to babysit this nutty bitch. She wanted Jake dead, and now this dumb kid was visiting her, confiding in her. He'd gone to Flint about this, but the old man ordered him to back off and just record the conversations. His hands were tied.

*　*　*

Later, as Jake left the prison corridor, Bex waited for him.

"So it's true," she began.

"Your dad must've told you."

"She tried to murder you, Jake! She's killed hundreds, maybe thousands of people. How can you willingly visit her?"

"You wouldn't understand."

"Try me."

They walked together, heading back toward the dorm rooms. "I have no illusions about her. I know she's a monster."

"Then why?"

"There are things no one understands about me, Bex."

"And she does? Give me a break. I've spent the last four months undoing the damage she did to her entire faction. It's brutal. And here you are, volunteering."

"It's not like that. I'm never alone; someone is always in the control room. I'm sorry you don't understand."

"You've got to stop this. Please. Please don't go to her anymore."

After a long silence, Jake said, "I can't promise that."

CHAPTER 22

Artemis opened his eyes. He blinked, stretched, and sat up in his hospital bed. Jake dozed in the armchair next to the bed, and a nurse checked on nearby patients. He couldn't quite recall how he'd ended up in here. He felt fine. Tip top, in fact.

"Jake," he nudged his friend. "Jake."

Jake stirred and jolted upright. Seeing Artemis awake brought a broad smile and a sigh of relief. "Holy shit! We thought we'd lost you."

"Aside from not knowing how I got here, I've never felt better."

"Nanos working overtime. Artemis, what's the last thing you remember doing?"

He pondered the question, falling silent.

Jake fired off a quick text.

Artemis' eyes suddenly flared with recognition. "I was following those bullies. They were in the staff area. I...just wanted to be helpful, to assist in your investigation. They must've seen me and lay in wait. They...you know, they actually attacked me from behind. The cowards." He shook his head.

"Who was in the group?"

"All the usual suspects. Oh, and that new boy, Dante. He was there."

"Of course."

"What could they be up to?" Artemis asked while stretching and working out the kinks from such a long rest.

98

"I wish I knew. This seems to be more than just their normal hooliganism."

"We've got to tell Dr. Flint right now."

The door at the end of the hall burst open, Trent and Bex soared through to get to their friends.

"Damnit, Artemis!" Bex exclaimed as she threw her arms around him. "Don't ever pull any stupid stunts like that again!"

Trent fist-bumped the kid. "Welcome back, sleepyhead."

Artemis filled the newcomers in on what had happened to him. "So, let us away to Flint's office, post-haste," he concluded.

Jake, Bex, and Trent exchanged cautious looks. Artemis noted it. "What are you not telling me?"

Trent spoke up. "Let's not be too quick on this."

"My dad hasn't been himself lately. I don't want to put too much on his plate."

"Yeah, I think we can handle this ourselves," Jake summed up.

"I may be young, but I am no fool. Tell me what's really going on."

"Fine," began Bex. "Something is off with my dad. I don't know if he's sick or stressed or what, but his sense of justice has been, I don't know, skewed lately. If we tell him what really happened…"

"Dr. Flint may go easy on them," added Jake.

"And then all we would have accomplished is showing our hand to those pricks," finished Trent.

"And forfeiting the element of surprise," concluded Artemis. "Well that's all you had to say."

The door opened once again. Sean Whitaker rushed to his son's side, followed closely by Dr. Flint and Jake's parents. Hugs were exchanged, but Dr. Flint kept his professional demeanor and distance. Stepping up to play his part, Artemis recounted the events for the adults, spinning a tale of looking for a book he wasn't supposed to have that led him to the forbidden staff lounge.

They bought it.

CHAPTER 23

January gave way to February, and the rains in Southern California seemed to wash away the blood and violence of the past few months. For the Phalanx headquarters, life had returned to normal. Neither a hint nor whisper of the murderer had been gleaned. The last group of former Hunter faction members was now deep into their deprogramming. Most of the factionless Mechcrafters had found homes in Phalanx or Gauntlet, and some had moved beyond the reach of the local factions.

The spring dance was now just one week away, and the planning committee had finalized their plans down to the single nano placement. The open arena in the center of the building, typically used for practice, would be transformed into a glorious metallic medieval fantasy setting—complete with dragons, knights, wizards, and of course, a queen and king.

Neera Bahar led the planning committee and couldn't be any more excited for this event. The darkness of the recent past needed to be dispelled. There was so much to look forward to, and she felt this dance would help usher in a new phase of positivity for her faction. Plus, Trent had asked her to the dance, the answer to a dream she'd cherished for over a year.

The student body seemed to have relaxed as attention spans shifted from the missing killer, to the upcoming event. Also, the reassurance of extra security patrols had helped put everyone at ease.

The adults, however, were given no such luxury. The faculty, field agents, and security all remained on heightened alert. The mimic incident at the warehouse had taught them all that the killer could be anywhere. Tina, Greg, and others still harbored concern over Flint's current state of mind, and why he was so hesitant to place the HQ on full lockdown.

Greg had even gone as far as secretly reaching out to Washington, going above Flint's head. Their response had been zero help: status quo. Flint would remain in charge unless formal complaints deemed otherwise.

Much to their frustration, the adults simply had to contend with Flint and his questionable decisions. Then there was the matter of Jake's private lessons with Flint. Jake assured them that nothing strange went on, and he was actually learning a lot. They allowed the lessons to continue, despite their growing misgivings.

Jake's visits to Sasha had ceased. As the deprogramming wound down and the losses and failed attempts to rescue her stranded faction were finally tallied, Jake couldn't bear to look her in the eye. His guilt was palpable. Plus, the strain his visits caused with Bex was not worth it.

Bex felt relief that her time as a deprogrammer was nearing an end. It meant Dante would be heading home to DC soon...hopefully. He had been a model citizen since his arrival, but that only creeped her out all the more. She knew him well enough to sense when he was plotting something.

In the cafeteria, Bex, Trent, Jake, Sophie, Neera, and Artemis picked at their lunches. While the rest of the students fixated on the upcoming festivities, the five of them felt the weight of current events upon their shoulders.

From the corner of her eye, Bex could see Dante and the bullies taking note of them, but none braved the walk over to their table.

Jake noted her glance over to Dante, as did Neera.

"Don't worry," he took her hand. "He'll be gone soon enough."

"I'm counting the days."

Trent, feeling the tension, attempted to lighten the mood. "So, Artemis. Which lucky girl is your date to the dance?"

"Oh...well...I haven't exactly asked anyone yet."

"We have to remedy that. Right, Bex?"

Bex snapped out of her funk, looking over to her young friend. "Absolutely. Operation Arti-date is in effect."

"No...no, please. I really don't want that."

"Let's get a list going," chimed in Trent. "Pros versus cons."

"You really don't have to," protested Artemis.

Sophie silently grinned at the teasing.

Ignoring Artemis' protestations, Bex rallied with Trent. "Portia Tanner. Shoni Williams."

"Zoe Barlow. Tracy Davis," added Neera.

Jake could see Artemis' embarrassment growing. "Alright, you two. Cool your jets. I'm pulling the plug on your plans."

"What? Why?" they exclaimed in unison.

"Clearly our friend can find his own date. Or better yet, he can go single, if he wants."

Artemis perked up at Jake's interference.

"What fun is that? He should let us set him up!" Bex urged.

"Thank you, but no thank you. My love life is no one else's concern."

"Fair enough," conceded Trent.

"You're no fun, but okay. Have it your way," added Bex.

Trent turned to Sophie, and opened his mouth, but she cut him off. "Don't even think about it, *omae*," she said flatly.

Trent smiled and backed off. "Fine, fine...whatever."

Dante watched Bex and her friends from afar. He still couldn't reconcile that she was with that freak. Mechcrafters were superior beings, disciplined and skilled. Jake's very existence went against everything Mechcraft stood for. How could everyone not see this? How could Flint accept this?

He had to expose this fraud. His intentions were partly selfish, he had to admit. As long as Jake was in the picture, he'd never have a chance with Bex. And what of Bex? Dante desired revenge against her just as much as he wanted her back. It was a true conflict within him. He loved her, but she really did need to pay for what she had done.

Greg and Tina couldn't resist doting over Jake. In light of the recent horrific events, they were grateful for their son's safety and felt compelled to fawn over him in a desperate attempt to keep his psyche healthy. Jake had seen and done things no person ever should have to, and they were terrified what damage was resulting from the excessive violence.

Plus, they'd be hard-pressed to admit it, but they carried a heavy dose of guilt for bringing him into this life in the first place. His DNA was beyond their control, but when he made the conversion and unleashed his nanotech, they could have kept it secret from Phalanx, from everyone.

Although, if they were honest in their thoughts, they had to accept that there truly was no way to keep Jake's Mechcraft a secret. Hell, his own best friend had been a damned spy.

So here they were, living a dangerous life and trying to keep their kid sheltered from it all, even though he was at the center of much of it. For now, they had him to dinner in their apartment in the Phalanx headquarters, and soaked up every moment.

Chinese take-out littered the table. The family favorite.

"Seems like you're fitting in much better now," commented Tina, Orange Chicken entering her mouth.

"Yes," agreed Greg. "Looks like keeping your ability in check seems to be working."

"But when I've used it, I've saved lives," protested Jake.

"And we're grateful it's been there for you," replied Greg, "but hiding the power back here in Phalanx has gone a long way to putting everyone at ease."

"I don't know. I still get stared at and avoided."

"Thankfully, you've got great friends," Tina offered.

"How's Bex doing?" Greg pivoted the discussion. "She happy the deprogramming is almost done?"

"Thrilled. I think she's ready to get back to her normal routine. She even said she wanted to get back out in the field."

"That's wonderful! Except for the field part. I can't believe Flint allows his own daughter to be exposed to so much danger," exclaimed Tina.

"She did get me safely here, and saved my life. She's really good at what she does."

"Even still. It's too much for a child...a teen...to have to bear."

Jake considered his mother's words and thought back to Bex's anxiety and stress. *Hard to argue her point.*

CHAPTER 24

The Spring dance filled the headquarters with excitement and anticipation. Students donned their best suits and dresses, adorning themselves in mech-created accessories. Each item showed flair and movement. A dozen strand necklace rotated and spun about the neck. A lapel pin shape-shifted from a rose to a sword to a mini dragon. Elaborate earrings danced on their hooks like puppets, and glittering tiaras hovered above lovingly styled hair. Every person desired to give the best show.

The faculty, security, and parents, on the other hand, roamed the halls and dance area with laser focus and an eye on everyone. They moved in threes over the entire facility. If Flint demanded the dance proceed, they would do their damnedest to make it safe.

The decorating committee had worked wonders with the open arena in the center of the building. Stunning colored mech piping and banners interlaced all the way up several stories, casting gorgeous hues of red, blue, and purple.

The medieval fantasy theme filled every inch of the space with the mech dragon moving along the walls, mech suits of armor standing guard at the entrance, and, of course, a detailed castle in the background of the stage.

The cafeteria had stepped up their game as well, leaving out a spread fit for royalty. Several meats, vegetable dishes, breads, and a mound of sweets adorned the buffet tables.

On the stage, as the students made their way in, a band set up for their gig. No outsiders could be allowed to play here, but, thankfully, Phalanx had their own resident rock band who were actually quite good at both covers and original songs. The foursome, two guys and two girls, busied themselves setting up guitars, drums, amps, and mics.

The band, Nanomare, slung their guitars over their shoulders as the drummer picked up sticks and sat behind his rig. With a hard strum on the lead guitar, they launched into their set, drawing the growing crowd of teens to the stage.

Arm in arm, Bex and Jake entered the dance, followed by Trent and Neera, and the solo Artemis. Jake felt relief as no one paid him any mind. He was just another student...for once.

If anything, all eyes landed on Bex, who looked stunning in her emerald dress. Her long, auburn hair cascaded down her back as dozens of tiny, crafted fairy lights danced in and out of the locks. She was radiant; the effect and her happiness was enchanting.

Shapely and tall, Neera also wowed in her sleek, black dress with just the right amount of bling. Her black hair was pulled up in an elegant design; a modest circlet of gently pulsing silver was woven into the crown. She was all about sophistication tonight, and Trent walked beside her like he'd won the lottery.

The gentlemen wore suits in matching shades to their dates, completing the ensembles. Artemis wore a black suit with intricate, constantly rotating mechs, gears and sprockets, interwoven on his vest. At one pocket, a luminous watch hung from a silver chain, the hands in constant anti-movement. He'd called forth images of Steampunk fashion in just the right measure.

And observing intensely from the corner, Dante and the bullies watched as their target strolled in without a care. "Asshole," whispered Dante, glaring at Jake.

Rick, Jonas, Mark, and Chloe had their own axes to grind with Jake, and they were only too happy to have Dante join them. He had a plan, and it sounded solid to them.

Sophie, who had received help with a dress from Bex, Neera, and some of the other girls, looked adorable in a sophisticated, pink and white A-line ensemble. Faint, aqua butterfly wings waved gently along her back; she'd never felt so elegant or grown up.

Eyes riveted to watch this strange young girl enter; she found Jake and his friends and joined them, smiling.

*   *   *

As the night wore on, the buffet table had been devoured, the punch bowls refilled twice, and now, most of the students clogged the dance floor as Nanomare broke into popular dance song covers.

Dancing with Bex, Jake was able to forget the troubles of the time, and simply be a teenager. He could see the joy on her face as well. Her stresses melted away, at least for now.

He loved Bex. Knew it in his very soul. This moment solidified the feeling...and such a simple thing, this dance. Yet living life and seeing her this happy in this moment brought it all home for him. They'd said the words before, and he truly felt the connection, however, the depth of that love revealed itself to him only now.

He leaned in and they kissed. He placed his hands on either side of her face as she wrapped her arms around him. The exchange was so passionate, others nearby stopped dancing, distracted by this powerful couple.

When at last their lips parted, the look in Bex's eyes told him she felt everything as he did. He saw their future together; in her eyes, he saw home.

The lovers didn't see the vile stare from Dante across the room. The other bullies were with him, but they busied themselves with other distractions. Only Dante was laser focused on the lovers.

Nanomare slowed things down with a ballad and the couples took over the floor. Trent and Neera, getting along very well, stepped next to Jake and Bex and slow danced along with them. While Trent and Jake exchanged looks of approval, Bex and Neera did the same. The soft glow of the colored mechs soaring and dipping above cast shades of blue, red, and purple over their faces, creating a surreal moment in time where nothing and everything seemed real.

Jake felt an inner peace, bliss like he'd never experienced before. Was this what a normal life could be like?

He glanced to his right and spied Artemis slow dancing with Sophie. He indicated the startling turn of events to Bex, who grinned endearingly.

The night was perfect.

*   *   *

As the evening wore on, Nanomare began their last set of the night. About half the teens were now seated, while the diehards still rocked the dance floor.

Jake, Trent, and Artemis downed punch and chatted at the buffet table while they waited for the girls to return from the restroom. In short notice, Bex, Neera, and Sophie re-entered the open area and headed back to their dates.

Without warning, Dante swept up to Bex and forced her into a dance twirl, bringing her in close as the music played on. Processing what had just occurred, she shoved him away hard.

"What the hell, Dante?" she yelled.

The bullies came up and stood behind Dante, a wall of support.

"Take it easy, darlin'," he responded. "Just messing around."

Bex could no longer stifle her rage toward him. Even though Dante had been on his best behavior, her intuition constantly nagged at her that he was plotting. And now she knew he was up to something.

"Stay the fuck away from me."

Jake saw the distressed look on Bex's face and rushed to her side, followed closely by Trent and Artemis.

"You okay?" Jake asked Bex.

"Your girlfriend's a psycho," interrupted Dante. "Attacked me for no reason."

"I'm fine," Bex focused on Jake. "He surprised me is all."

"We saw the whole thing. You shoved Dante," exclaimed Chloe. Rick, Jonas, and Mark nodded their agreement.

"*What?*" Bex exclaimed, incredulous.

Dante adjusted his tie and jacket. "It's alright. I'm alright. Take it easy, Bex. You need to get ahold of yourself."

"Go to hell."

Jake stepped between Bex and Dante, facing down the asshole ex-boyfriend. "Leave her alone," he grunted.

Dante threw up his hands in mock surrender. "Hey, I'm not starting shit. I'm the victim here."

Jonas chimed in, "He was minding his own business."

"Bex assaulted Dante," added Chloe.

Rick and Mark again nodded in support of their friends.

"I call bullshit," interjected Trent.

Artemis couldn't help noticing the excited expression Sophie wore. *Was she actually thrilled at this turn of events and the promise of violence?*

"Back off, Trent. You're not in this," barked Chloe.

To Dante, Jake said, "Enough. Take your minions and get away from us. And do not ever speak to Bex again."

"Or what, Jake?" he taunted. "You gonna blow up our mechs? Or better yet take control of them and shove 'em up our asses?"

Jake wanted nothing more than to grant Dante's request, but his parents' words bludgeoned his brain. He had to keep his cool, conceal his power, hide his true self.

"Not going to happen, Dante."

Jake turned and took Bex's hand. She smiled at him uneasily, as he began to lead her away from the confrontation.

Trent, Artemis, Neera, and Sophie took their cue and moved in the same direction as Jake and Bex.

Dante glanced at Chloe, and gave a slight nod. She grinned in response.

"This is over," began Jake to his friends. "Come on, guys."

But before the group could step away from the confrontation, Chloe summoned and unleashed a mech whip-like tendril, snapping it at Artemis—slicing his cheek.

It was the spark in the powder keg and the dynamite blew. In unison, the friends leaped into action. An attack on their most vulnerable would not stand. Bex pulled Artemis behind her, out of harm's way. Sophie conjured her trademark oversized mech mallet. Neera summoned a mech shield around Artemis and Bex. Trent created and sent large tentacles whipping at Dante and Chloe. Jake could only call out for them to stop, but it was too late.

Dante conjured his own tentacles to block and counter Trent's. Chloe recalled her nanos and began conjuring again. Rick fired small, dangerous spheres from his palms at the entire group of enemies. Jonas generated a staff and swung it at Jake, who ducked just in time. Mark conjured a knife and stalked around his friends toward his target: Jake.

Sophie leaped into the air and swung her giant mallet, knocking Chloe aside and disrupting her conjurations. Trent telepathically commanded his tentacles to overpower Dante's. Mark ran up on Jake and jabbed his mech knife at his exposed ribs, only to be met with a mech-coated torso Jake had quietly summoned over himself. The knife bent, and Jake decked Mark across the face.

Phalanx staff began rushing over to the melee, including Greg, Tina, and Grant.

Trent withdrew his nanos to conjure a new mech, leaving Dante's tentacles free to move. He grabbed the opportunity and used the mechs to pull down Neera's shield, exposing Bex and Artemis.

With the fight escalating, Trent opted for a more deadly mech, summoning a handful of levitating, razor-sharp blades. Jake, horrified, noted the shift in Trent's tactic.

"Trent, don't!"

Too late; Trent sent the deadly weapons at the unsuspecting bullies. They would be seriously wounded, or worse. And Trent would be severely punished, maybe expelled. The bullies would win.

Against all rules, against all he'd been told, Jake concentrated and destroyed all the mechs in his immediate area. Every nano-built creation, all the weapons, shields, and even floating decorations vaporized into a chrome mist.

Everyone witnessed the event. Nanomare stopped playing. The dancers turned to stare; the seated party-goers gawked, openmouthed.

Dante saw his chance just as the staff arrived and pretended to fall back into his friends. "Jake, stop! Don't hurt me anymore!" Dante cried.

As the nano-mist separated and returned to their owners, the staff got between the enemy groups. Greg and Tina stood next to Jake.

Dante wasn't finished. The entire room was fixated on them.

"See!" he yelled. "He doesn't belong here. He's dangerous and unpredictable!"

Grant took position in front of Dante, glaring at him, seeing through his bullshit.

"That's enough out of you," he grunted at the student.

Dante quieted down, his damage already done.

The student body wore expressions ranging from anger to terror. Acceptance of Jake's presence was already tenuous, and this incident was all it took to sway the student body against this freak.

Trent assessed the situation they suddenly found themselves in, and sighed.

"Well, it was fun while it lasted."

CHAPTER 25

Dr. Flint leaned back in his office chair, hands folded, expression deep in thought. Across the desk from him sat Jake and Trent. Behind them stood Artemis, Neera, Bex, and Sophie. Near the door, in the background, stood Greg, Tina, and Grant. All waited in anticipation for Flint to speak.

"Unacceptable," he finally said. "This entire situation is unacceptable. Jake, you were told never to use your unique powers in the view of the students. You were supposed to maintain your private lessons under my care. And Trent, I expected an older student such as yourself to be a better example."

Greg moved to protest, but Tina rested her hand on his arm, gently encouraging him to hold back for now.

Dr. Flint continued. "We cannot risk such an incident again. You are all suspended from any functions or extra activities beyond your lessons and meal times."

Bex had had enough. "*Us*? You're punishing us? What about those assholes who started it?"

"Calm down, daughter. They have been removed. You won't see them again."

"That's what you said last time," Bex fired back.

"And that was an error I don't plan on making again. Still, my requirement of you five stands."

"For how long?" asked Trent.

"I think two weeks, perhaps a month ought to be enough time for this to blow over in the public eye."

Trent scoffed. "And what about the investigation? I've been deep into this since day one."

"And you shall return to working on it as soon as your discipline is over."

Grant stepped forward. "Max, come on. We need him. He's an integral member of—"

"My decision is final on this, Grant."

"Sidelining me is not the way to handle this!" fumed Trent.

"My methods will not be questioned," Flint calmly replied.

Greg spoke up. "Isolating these kids is not going to fix anything or make the rest of the students less fearful. Bex, Neera, and Artemis were not even part of the fight. There's no reason to do this to them. And Trent is vital to finding the murderer. And, there's something else, Max. Jake needs to be seen *more* by the other students, not less."

Dr. Flint rose from his chair, and casually walked to the door. "Noted. Now if you'll please excuse me, I have work to attend to."

He held the door open for the group, indicating the meeting was over.

They made their way out of the office, dumbfounded by Flint's decision and the finality of it. Bex couldn't even look him in the eye as she passed. Her father was no longer the man she'd known her whole life. A stranger was playing stand in.

What's wrong with him?

* * *

The next few days proved rough. At the direction of Greg and Tina, the students obeyed Flint's odd detention regiment. It didn't help matters at all.

Jake was once more looked upon with suspicion and fear by nearly every Mechcrafter he passed or sat near. Some turned their gaze from him, others steered clear altogether. At least he had Trent as a roommate, mutually commiserating their misfortune.

Trent became restless, not being able to assist in the ongoing investigation. He was letting Grant and the team down. His bitterness toward Dr. Flint grew by the day. He owed the man so much, yet his actions lately clearly showed the serious changes in the good doctor.

Neera and Bex busied themselves with closing out all the files and documents on their long list of deprogrammed Hunter agents. Their pride in their success was overshadowed by the knowledge that Dante had assisted, and by Dr. Flint's bizarre punishment. They worked mostly in silence, joining the adult deprogrammers in the shutting down of the offices.

Artemis, feeling completely exposed and vulnerable since his friends became sidelined, was all too happy going straight to his room after classes and meals. Even though the bullies had been expelled, for real this time, he couldn't shake a subtle foreboding that followed him everywhere. Something was amiss.

* * *

Under Timothy James' leadership, the Gauntlet faction had fallen into disarray. His promises of glory and dominance had enticed a large enough segment of their soldiers to mutiny against Grant MacReady.

Timothy, drunk with power, ruled with tribal, warmongering sensibilities, but his leadership skills were weak. The hierarchy was blurred, and without an established structure. Protocol was out the window, and the well-oiled machine of the Gauntlet soldiers fell into selfishness and chaos. Supplies dwindled. Process fell to randomness.

And the soldiers were pissed. None more than advisor, Bea Moreno. She loved Grant as a friend and leader, but had lost confidence in him once he'd become enamored with Jake London and the truce with Phalanx. Grant had put her in a tough spot, forcing her to choose loyalty to him or serving the needs of the faction. In the end, she had felt Timothy could lead them and sided with him. That decision turned out to be the greatest regret of her life.

Timothy's arrogance and short-sighted vision was bringing the faction to its breaking point. All he focused on now was arresting Grant and crushing Phalanx. She knew he had plans for Jake, but was keeping those to himself.

In the war room, she persisted, even though her pleas fell on deaf ears. "Another brawl between the soldiers today. Five this time," she reported.

"Stop wasting my time with this bullshit. Report on Grant," Timothy ordered.

"He has gone to ground; no sign of him anywhere. Obviously he's taken refuge at the Phalanx HQ."

"It's been long enough. I'm tired of waiting. Let's send a delegation to pay our new friends a visit."

"Are you sure that's wise? We're experiencing a difficult...transition period."

"Stop contradicting me, Bea!" he barked. "I will not be questioned. Just send a dozen soldiers, and go yourself."

"Fine. I'll make the arrangements."

CHAPTER 26

"I assure you," began Dr. Flint, leaning forward in his office chair. "We have not seen nor heard from Grant MacReady. And if we do, we absolutely will contact you."

Bea Moreno knew he was lying, and poorly, but she had to play the game. Unlike Timothy, she was not chomping at the bit to go to war with Phalanx.

"Thank you, doctor," she replied calmly. "We appreciate your effort. MacReady is a fugitive and must be apprehended."

"What is his crime?"

"Excuse me?"

"With this level of manhunt, his crime must have been severe."

"Oh. Yes. He...violated our code and sabotaged several important missions. Definitely an unstable man."

"A hero from Disruption Day fallen so far so fast?"

"Times are changing, doctor. It's a mad world these days."

"Seems like I need to get out more."

*   *   *

In the lobby outside Flint's office, Bea's escort, six Gauntlet soldiers, waited for her meeting to conclude. They stood at ease, but none wandered or meandered, or even looked aside.

Flint's office manager sat at his desk observing the disciplined stance of the visitors. They seemed unreasonably tense. He made a mental note to report this oddity to Dr. Flint.

*　*　*

In Jake and Trent's dorm room, Bex and Grant sat with the boys. The mood was somber.

"Even though we've seen no activity from the killer since the warehouse," began Grant, "I'm sure none of us believes it's over."

"Agreed," said Trent. "But can't really do anything about it, handcuffed to our room."

"Dad's decision is completely ridiculous. I don't understand him anymore. He's like a stranger to me." The change in Dr. Flint weighed heaviest on his daughter.

"I'm all for sneaking out of here to do what we need to do, but, if we're caught, then it's more isolation time. Do we risk it?" Jake asked.

"That's for you guys to decide, but I'd love the help," said Grant. "The Phalanx agents are great, but I consider us the true team leading this investigation. And with Gauntlet on the hunt for me, it's tough to show my face outside these walls. Basically, I'm a prisoner here, too. Hell, my own soldiers are in this building as we speak asking Flint about me. I only hope he doesn't rat me out."

Bex sighed. "A year ago I'd have said that would never happen, but with the way he's been acting, nothing would surprise me."

"Do you think he's sick? Or maybe at the start of something like dementia or Alzheimer's?" asked Trent.

"I've asked if he's well, but he waves it away. Won't discuss anything with me anymore."

Jake added, "I know my parents and most of the staff are growing tired of this. Not sure if they're talking about a mutiny yet, though."

"I wouldn't blame them at all," stated Grant. "But it's so political. No one wants a spotlight on their headquarters from the bosses in DC. That just begs a visit from them, or worse—a takeover. Nobody wants them running things directly."

"I'm sure they'll handle this in-house," added Trent.

"For now, what do we do?" Bex moved the conversation along.

Grant rose. "I'll keep with the team and bide my time for your release from the penalty box."

"We'll investigate within the building as best we can," said Jake.

"Taking only reasonable risks," added Trent. "Much to my disappointment."

CHAPTER 27

Scott Berg wandered the halls of Phalanx. It had been just under a month since disavowing his Hunter loyalty. He found a mixture of relief and grief in this severing of ties.

For the most part, the Phalanx agents, staff, and most students had forgiven his participation related to the events of Disruption Day and his role in exposing Jake to Sasha. His life now was a picture of normalcy: classes, video games, Mechcraft practice—which had improved his feeble skill greatly—the Spring dance, and just hanging out.

However, he could not escape the guilt over what he'd done. The deprogrammers blamed it on Sasha's cult-like influence over him, but he knew it was not so simple. Orphaned and living on the streets of Los Angeles, Scott had been welcomed in by Sasha, who'd promised a great life. All he needed to do was accept the gift. Starved and cold, Scott had not been able to resist the golden prize she offered.

Yet, after enduring the Mechcraft injections, her attitude towards him shifted; he became just another follower under her rule. He had desperately wanted her approval and love, and he worked so hard to gain it from her. All his efforts had been in vain, until she needed a teenager to keep an eye on a potential Mechcrafter in Orange County.

His friendship with Jake fell naturally into place, and he found that he really did like this guy. He held onto hope that whatever indicator

Sasha was looking for in Jake would never show up, and he could simply remain his friend.

Then that fateful night when Jake made the transformation. Scott heard the whole thing play out over his headset as the Mechcraft had burst from Jake's body. He had hesitated at first. A small part of him had been tempted to ignore the event and carry on without informing his master.

But when he heard Sasha's voice in his head, all the love and appreciation for him in her words and tone, he found that he craved that attention more than he valued the friendship with Jake. He was all in with Sasha.

Now, knowing full well the pain and loss he'd caused, especially to Jake, he could barely bring himself to rise in the morning. Jake and his friends wanted nothing to do with him. He understood, and, frankly, was surprised they hadn't killed him on sight.

In all of Phalanx, there was only one person he could turn to for acceptance, approval and love: Sasha.

He stood at the guard station in front of the cell area, security blocking the path.

"I just need a few minutes with Sasha," he pleaded.

Security, stoic as ever, replied, "You'll need approval from Dr Flint."

"I understand, but if you could bend the rules just this once—"

"No former Hunters are permitted to see Sasha. Move along. Now."

Dejected, Scott stepped away and continued aimlessly down the halls. He found himself near the faculty corridors, but kept going, knowing he'd eventually end up at the cafeteria. A movement down a side hall caught his eye, and he looked to his right. He saw a face he never expected.

Dante Barnes opened a door to the staff lounge and slipped in quietly. *What's he doing here? I thought they were expelled.*

He had to tell someone immediately. Then it dawned on him: this could be a start to redeeming himself with Jake. He rushed off.

* * *

Bex sat in her room alone. She had been dressing for the day, but anxiety overtook her in a surprise attack, and she couldn't stop shaking. Her hands trembled and she sobbed uncontrollably.

She took deep breaths, trying to get ahold of herself. She thought she'd moved past this, after the breakthrough in the control room. Sadly, she was still very much under the ruthless control of her PTSD, and now felt maybe she always would be.

Her breathing at last normalized, and her shakes subsided. Neera would be waiting for her; she coated her hands in green apple-scented sanitizer, and steeled herself for the day.

* * *

Unable to concentrate on work, Bea Moreno left her quarters and knocked on Timothy James' door.

"Yes?" came the response from the other side.

"It's Bea," she began. "We need to talk."

Still not opening the door, Timothy replied, "What about? I'm very busy."

"About this path against Phalanx you've got us on. Look, just open the door."

"I'm too busy to deal with your doubts today."

She knocked again. Louder. "Open the door," she grunted.

"I advise you to leave. I'm not in the mood for this bullshit."

"Fine," she sighed, "but we're not done talking about this."

As she stormed away, fuming, she did not see the puddle of liquid silver slowly undulating on the ceiling, coming from the top seam of the door to Tim's room.

CHAPTER 28

Keeping things as routine as possible, Jake dined with his parents in their apartment. As they dished out lasagna and salad, the casual conversation eventually gave way to more pressing matters.

"What are you guys going to do about Dr. Flint?" asked Jake just before chomping a large bite of warm garlic bread.

"Nothing. Nothing at all," retorted Tina.

"He's making questionable decisions, but he's still our leader and boss," summarized Greg.

"But his behavior—"

"It's actually for us to handle, Jake. You don't need to be concerned," continued Greg.

"No. I'm not on board with that. We said no more secrets, remember?"

They both sighed. He was right.

"Fine. You're right. Truth is, the staff are very worried. We are formulating a contingency plan, should he go further off the rails. But you are not to be involved in any way. Do not talk about this outside this apartment please."

"I understand. Thank you for trusting me."

"We do trust you, and want to keep open communication with you," said Tina, "but we also want to keep you safe...or at least try to."

"And we need you to trust us as well. Trust us with your reasons for visiting Sasha. Why do you go to her, of all people?"

Jake tensed. He hadn't expected a direct query about this.

"I'm not hiding anything," he began. "All our conversations are recorded as part of the agreement."

"We know. And we've heard them," Tina said. "The content, while interesting, is not where we have questions. It's the 'why' of it all."

Greg jumped in. "After what she's done to you, to all of us.... Why would you want to go to her?"

Jake sighed. "I don't know if you'll understand."

"No more secrets, right?"

"Right. Well, despite all she put us through, we share a connection; she has an understanding of me that no one else does."

He noted the worried looks on their faces.

"Believe me. I don't like it. And I despise her. But all that aside, our talks have helped me. In that capacity, at least, she's doing some good."

"What connection could you possibly share with her?" asked Greg.

"You've heard the recordings."

"But Jake, she's so dangerous. Her words are as deadly as her skill," Tina fretted.

"And she doesn't have either anymore. She doesn't hold any influence over me. You can hear it in the tapes. And Ben is always there in the command center. I'm never truly alone with her."

"Fair enough," sighed Greg.

"Speaking of Ben," began Tina, "...haven't seen him in a few days."

"I'd say maybe he called out sick, but we don't get sick," said Greg.

* * *

In the cafeteria, Bex and Neera dined alone, not in the mood to be social with the other students. Given their friendship with Jake, they sensed the student body was happy to keep their distance from them as well. Fear by association.

"Have you seen Trent since the dance?" asked Bex.

"No. Couple of texts, but nothing much," Neera sounded disappointed.

"Sorry my dad pulled this detention crap."

"Me too. I think Trent and I could be good together, you know? And I hate waiting to find out."

Artemis and Sophie approached, trays of food in their hands. They sat with Bex and Neera.

"What's all this moping around for?" asked Sophie with too much spunk in her tone.

Neera chimed in quick. "Nothing. Just anxious for this punishment to end."

"I hear ya," Sophie replied. "I miss the practice ring. Reminds me of the warehouse."

"And I miss the library," added Artemis.

Bex didn't verbalize her feelings, but she missed Jake. Sure, they saw each other at mealtime and class time, but she ached to be with him on their own time. A few stolen kisses and hand holding was not enough.

CHAPTER 29

Dr. Flint no longer needed to visit the entity in the basement. His thoughts were its thoughts. They were connected on a deeper level than before. He no longer dreaded the thing, but embraced it and all its machinations. Obedience was easy when in complete agreement.

Having sent the Gauntlet team away, he knew what needed to be done when dealing with them. Grant still had his uses, so he had decided not to hand him over. He also desired to maintain the appearance of an alliance with the other faction, even though he saw them as his only real threat now. They would be dealt with soon enough.

He pondered his plans as he made his way to Sasha's containment area.

Jake had made a few visits to her, and each session had proved to be an insightful look into the boy's psyche. His lessons were going well, but he needed an edge to bring Jake closer to him. Trust was the desired outcome. Jake was the prototype for a whole new direction for Phalanx; the kid just didn't know it yet.

In the command center, Flint came upon agent Sara Goldman where Ben Donovan should have been. Flint didn't think anything of the change. He simply greeted her and proceeded to meet with Sasha.

He pulled up the chair and sat facing the clear cell.

Sasha, seated in a fetal position, knees pulled close to her chin, noticed the doctor and slowly moved toward him. Her captor rarely came to see her anymore.

"What do you want?" she hissed.

"Sasha, we were close once. My star pupil. Surely you can find an ounce of courtesy...for old times' sake?"

"Oh, is that how we're playing today? Kiss my ass...sir."

"Feisty to the end. I always liked that about you."

"Cut the small talk, doc. As you can see, I'm very busy."

"I want to know why Jake is visiting you."

"Why should I tell you?"

"Truly, you have no reason to help me at all. However, it seems you've developed a fondness for him. I believe you are actually trying to help him understand and cope with the knowledge of who he is. I applaud your efforts. I'm also trying to help him. I thought perhaps we could exchange notes and ideas to better assist him."

"*You* want to team up with *me*? Don't make me laugh. You don't want to help Jake. You want to contain him...or...is it that you have some use for him?"

"Teaching him control of his power is hardly containment."

"He needs to be practicing those powers, exploring them. You have no idea what he really is."

"And you do? Making him a pawn in your conquest was helping him? Making him a murderer was your big plan for this gifted kid? Don't lecture me on how best to help Jake."

"That's not me anymore."

"No. Now you're incarcerated for the mass murder of hundreds of innocent lives."

"Thanks for the reminder, doc. I almost forgot."

"I just thought perhaps you'd want your miserable life to have some semblance of meaning. Help me with Jake and obtain that meaning. Show us all that it wasn't a waste. That *you* aren't a waste."

"Your motivational speeches always inspired," she snapped sarcastically. "I'm not going to betray Jake. Show yourself out."

With that, she turned and gave Dr. Flint her back.

* * *

Having struck a dead end on the SUV plates from the zoo crime scene, Michael Ash switched his focus back to the woman at the Roxy. Using police station software, he brought clarity to a grainy, still image of a woman, taken off security cam footage from a blue-line train station in south Los Angeles the night of the train derailment tragedy.

No resolution had been discovered to explain why the train had jumped the track, killing 154 and injuring another 326.

While no footage existed of the crash itself, the reports of violence on the platform minutes prior had garnered two, distant, badly-focused video segments of a confrontation between two groups of people. In the brief clip, a woman in black appeared to be the leader of the approaching group.

Michael was willing to bet this was the woman from the Roxy.

He and the police IT person, Joe somebody, worked diligently to enhance and clarify the best still image they hijacked from the video. They'd spent hours playing with lighting, hue, removing the background noise, adding sharpness.

Unfortunately, all onboard security cameras had been destroyed, either in the crash or by the woman and her team using their strange powers. Of course, he could never mention this angle to his peers or his boss. He'd be locked in a padded cell.

Even if he could somehow link this woman and the others to the crimes at the Roxy and the train derailment, he wouldn't. For now, this was his secret. His project. He had to deal with them on his own. They provided something he desperately needed: a purpose.

Finally, after a few last tweaks, the figure became somewhat clear: it was the woman from the Roxy fight. She and her people were at the train station minutes before the tragedy.

He had to find her.

CHAPTER 30

Finding Ben Donovan missing from his post once again, Greg and Tina took it upon themselves to pay him a visit at his apartment.

They knocked on the door. No answer. Knocked again.

They looked at each other inquisitively. Without discussing their next move, Greg summoned a thin tentacle, causing Tina to smile because that's exactly what she would have done. He sent the small mech into the door's keyhole, and, in moments, the door swung gently open.

"Ben," Greg called. "You home?"

"Sorry to barge in," added Tina. "Everyone's worried about you. Are you okay?"

They were met with silence. The living room and kitchen were empty. No mess. No food left out. He kept a tidy apartment.

In the bedroom they found him. Ben Donovan lay motionless on his bed, eyes staring blankly at his visitors.

"Oh god!" exclaimed Tina.

Greg rushed to the lifeless body to check vitals. He pressed two fingers against Ben's cold neck, expecting no pulse, and receiving none.

Then they saw the cause. Partially covered by the bedsheet, a gaping wound engulfed most of Ben's shirtless torso. Although Greg and Tina had not witnessed the previous murder victims from Grant's investigation, his description of the bodies held true for Ben's. The wound looked as if something had exploded out of him from within. Blood caked the mattress, but no dead nanos were visible.

Tina stepped into the other room and immediately called the security office.

As Tina urgently informed security of the situation, Greg continued to scan the body. A faint liquid sound from above, barely audible, drew his attention. He glanced upward to see a large portion of the bedroom ceiling coated in thin liquid chrome, undulating like the surface of a pool.

He opened his mouth to shout a warning to his wife, but a wiry, lightning-fast tendril shot forth from the metallic pool and entered his mouth. He gasped and grabbed the metal tendril as it began to flail him about like a fish caught on a line. The attacking appendage spread itself out and coated Greg's face. He tried to scream as the liquid invaded his ears and eyes.

Tina ended her call and returned to the bedroom to find the ghastly display. She immediately conjured five razor-thin discs and launched them at the tendril. The blades each targeted the same spot, slicing deeper with each hit until, at last, the tendril severed, releasing Greg, who stumbled to the ground. The nanos encompassing his head immediately returned to their liquid state and rejoined their collective, writhing on the ceiling.

It fired another vine-like tendril at them, but Greg scrambled to his feet in time to dodge the attack. Tina pulled him away and got them the hell out of the bedroom. As she slammed the door, several attacks from the being struck it.

She helped her disoriented husband toward the living room, noting the liquid chrome seeping through the edges of the door and reforming on the ceiling.

In moments, the thing had pushed through the narrow space and had filled the ceiling once again. Tina and Greg stumbled into the living room, watching as the enemy slithered along above them in pursuit.

The couple prepared to summon defenses as the front door burst open and five security officers stormed in. They expected a body, not a fight, but even with the shocking turn of events, were able to conjure weapons right away. Assessing the situation, they cleared a path to allow Tina to help Greg out the door.

The chrome pool on the ceiling halted its attack when the officers entered. It moved slightly to the left, then right, as if pondering its next move.

Security didn't wait for an answer. They launched their attacks of spikes and blades. The ranged weapons seemed to have no effect on the being, but it elected to flee all the same. The team could only watch as the chrome pool melted into the ceiling and vanished.

The lead contacted the office to send more. They now had a manhunt to add to the crime scene.

*   *   *

Scott sheepishly knocked on Jake's door. Jake opened the door, took one look at him, and said, "I have nothing to say to you."

Scott pressed on. "I know you hate me. You have every reason to. But I have to tell you something."

"I don't want to hear anything you have to say, Scott. Just leave."

"Please. It's important. I wouldn't come here like this if it wasn't."

"Fine. What is it?"

"Last night, I was walking near the faculty halls, and I saw Dante fucking Barnes."

"Wrong. He and those other assholes have been expelled."

"Nope. It was him. He slipped into the staff lounge room."

The same place where Artemis was attacked. Had flint lied about removing them? Jake descended into thoughts on the implications of this. He almost forgot Scott was standing there.

"You okay?" asked Scott. "You kinda checked out on me."

"I'm good," he lied. "Thanks for the info."

"No problem. While I have you, I was hoping we could...talk this out sometime."

"Yeah, that's never going to happen," Jake quipped and shut his door.

Scott hung his head and wandered the halls alone.

Inside the dorm room, Trent asked, "He's trying."

"And?"

"Think you might give him a break? You've seen firsthand how bad Sasha messed with their heads. You've forgiven the other Hunters, why not Scott?"

"He set all this in motion. He caused it all. I can never forgive that."

Another knock at the door. Jake angrily opened it, and said, "Look, Scott, I already told—"

The sight of Neera Bahar stopped his speech cold.

"I don't know who Scott is, but I'm really glad I'm not him," said Neera with a grin and her charming British accent.

"Oh, sorry about that," he said, slightly embarrassed.

Trent came to the door. "Neera? How did you—"

"Can't a girl sneak out on detention? I got tired of waiting, so here I am."

Jake and Trent moved aside to let her in.

"I am definitely impressed," said Trent.

"Well, you don't get to be the only scoundrel in the building," she quipped.

Trent looked to Jake. "Don't you have that thing?"

Getting the picture, Jake said, "Oh, yeah...yes. I was just heading to the shower."

He stepped into the bathroom, leaving Trent and Neera alone.

She immediately flung herself into his arms, and they kissed with the passion only new love can inspire.

"I really missed you," he said between kisses.

"Me too."

They finally separated and sat on his bed.

"What do you think about what I texted?" he asked.

"It's a big step, but I'm in. I'm all in!"

"Then in just a few months, we'll be free of all this."

"We can go wherever we want."

"We could use the break."

"But what about Bex and Jake?"

"They'll be fine. They have each other. And it's not like this will be goodbye forever. It's your parents I'm more concerned about."

"We're waiting till I'm eighteen, so it won't matter what they say."

"Still, though, I'm sure I'm not their favorite, and I don't want to stack the deck against me even more."

"For a scoundrel, you worry way too much!" Neera took his hand, and added, "Trust me; we need this time away from it all."

*   *   *

Grant took Phalanx agents, Leo and Anne, out of the building to further the investigation. He intended to go back over the safe houses once again to see if there were any clues they might have missed. Even though the places had been swept by the Phalanx cleaning crew to avoid any police entanglements, Grant still wanted to double check.

He had no way of knowing that, as he ventured out on this mission, Ben Donovan's body was being discovered by Greg and Tina.

"Are you sure this is a good idea?" asked Anne. Everyone knew Gauntlet was actively looking for Grant.

"No risk, no reward."

"Fair enough."

They rolled up to the Pasadena house in the afternoon sun. Most people were still at their day jobs, so the street was deserted. The three walked around to the back and entered through the door, away from any prying eyes on the street.

The dim kitchen and living room remained untouched following the clean-up efforts. Grant, Anne, and Leo scoured the downstairs for anything out of the ordinary: broken window sills, moldings or door jambs, marks on the hardwood flooring, any small clue that someone else had overlooked. They checked the ceiling for damage, and likewise the furniture.

They moved upstairs. Anne went first, and when she reached the top landing, two, foot-long mech spikes soared down the hallway and pierced her torso, knocking her to the ground.

Leo reached the landing, conjuring a mech shield, and spied two men in military camouflage at the end of the hall, standing in the entry to the master bedroom. They launched more spikes, but they were deflected by the shield.

Grant pushed past Leo, saw his Gauntlet soldiers, and summoned his own shield. He looked down and saw that Anne was conscious and okay.

"Stand down!" ordered Grant.

"You aren't in command anymore, *sir*," came the cold reply.

"It's not too late," Grant pleaded. "We can all still walk away from this as if it never happened."

"Why would we want to do that? You betrayed us. Sold us out to the Phalanx suck-ups."

"That's Timothy's bullshit. Don't believe it."

"Sorry, Grant. It's over for you."

And with that, both soldiers launched a barrage of spikes, some penetrating the shields.

"Get her out of here!" yelled Grant, and then increased the size of his shield to encompass the entire hallway—protection for his companions.

Leo sprang into action, using his nanos to lift Anne and levitate her down the stairs.

"Don't wait for me. Get back to the base," he called after them.

"We're not leaving you," replied Leo.

"Don't worry about me. Get back to Phalanx. I'll be right behind you."

The soldiers battered the shield with mech sledgehammers, denting and tearing it.

Leo obeyed and assisted Anne out of the house.

Grant surprised his foes by bending the shield back onto them. They scrambled back and away just before being caught under the metallic blanket. He recalled his nanos and prepared to strike again. One soldier fired two tentacles, aiming for Grant's legs. The other attempted to distract him by pelting him with dozens of small spheres.

Grant didn't take the bait, countering the tentacles by conjuring and dropping a solid metal block on them—stopping them cold. He took several hits from the spheres, all minor wounds. "I am not your enemy."

"Our orders state otherwise."

Grant converted his solid block back to liquid and sent it splashing across the floor, coating the soldiers' boots. He immediately commanded the liquid to harden, locking them in place.

"Stop this now. I'll go with you back to base and speak with Timothy. It's time we cleared this up."

"You don't get it," began one soldier. "The mission is not to bring you in alive."

Those words sank in deep and hard. *They want me dead? My own faction has a hit out on me?*

The soldiers struggled and fought against their trapped feet.

"Sorry to disappoint you guys, but I'm not dying today."

Before the soldiers could react, Grant sent two thick tentacles at their heads, knocking both unconscious. He recalled his mechs and searched their pockets. Finding Humvee keys, he raced out of the house.

Outside, he clicked the alarm, hoping to discover the vehicle's location. Luck was with him as a standard alarm beep rang from inside the garage that stood a short distance from the back door. He drove away fast.

Despite the target on him now, he refused to kill any of his own. The soldiers would wake up with a headache, but at least they'd wake up.

It was time to confront his usurpers. Timothy seemed beyond reason, but he may be able to get through to Bea. Returning to his base might be the most foolish thing he'd ever do in his life, but it might also save them all from another war.

* * *

Wrapped up in his thoughts, Grant hadn't noticed the generic sedan following him from the Pasadena house.

In the car, Michael Ash pondered his quarry as he followed.

Why the camo uniforms? Were these soldiers? Army? Special Ops maybe? How were they involved in this?

Through patience and perseverance, Michael had scoured dozens of hours of camera footage from traffic intersection cams to business CCTV to neighborhood smart doorbell cams. The woman's image had turned up in four locations, several times. He had her. It had been just a matter of staking out the right home.

Pasadena had been second on his list.

CHAPTER 31

The alarm sounded throughout the entire Phalanx building. At first, the students and staff paused, unsure if this was real or a drill or a malfunction. But seconds later, teachers led their students out of classrooms; staff led the way from the cafeteria, and knocked on dorm doors.

Everyone began to gather in the open center of the building. Quickly, over three hundred people were huddled, discussing the possibilities.

Greg and Tina helped organize the security staff, sending them to various key points in the building.

Dr. Flint, having ignored the calls from security, stormed up to the couple. "What the hell is going on?" he shouted. "What's the meaning of this?"

Tina fired back, "If you'd answered your phone you'd know that Ben Donovan's been murdered. We're putting Phalanx on lockdown. We've notified DC as well."

"You had no authority to do that," he grunted.

"When everyone is accounted for, we'll begin evacuation," said Greg, ignoring Flint's indignation.

"You can't do this!"

"It's done," replied Greg.

"Max, as our friend, either help us or go sit in the crowd," added Tina.

Flint's outrage rendered him speechless. All he could manage to do was step away from them, dumbfounded.

* * *

Jake, Trent, and Neera moved from the dorm room into the open area to join Jake's parents. Bex, Artemis, and Sophie were not far behind. Greg and Tina updated them on the murder of Ben Donovan and the lockdown.

Having endured two encounters with the killer already, Sophie began shaking visibly. Artemis placed a reassuring arm around her as she whimpered.

"It's going to be okay," he said, trying to comfort her.

"We're here, and we look out for each other," added Trent.

"And we have Jake," said Bex. "If anything can stop this thing, he can."

Jake didn't care for the spotlight, but if it calmed Sophie's fear, then he'd endure it. In fact, in this state of emergency, he noticed everyone had forgotten their disdain and mistrust for him. Apparently, he was all good now in their eyes. He did his best not to be bitter about their convenient turn around.

Neera kissed Trent and hugged Bex then left to join her parents in the crowd.

Jake then caught Trent gazing about the arena intently. "Hey, what are you looking for?" he asked.

Trent reluctantly pulled his attention to Jake, and uttered, "If Scott is telling the truth and Dante and those assholes are still in the building, then why aren't they out here? If we're on lockdown, that means everyone. Even the prisoners. So if they're here, even in secret, Flint should have them in with all of us."

"What are you suggesting?" he asked, already knowing the answer.

"Let's go hunting."

* * *

Grant hung up the phone. Greg had filled him in on the Phalanx emergency. He desperately wanted to turn the Humvee around and help his friends, but kept his course. This confrontation with Timothy and Bea would pay off for Phalanx in the end. He would stay on task and join them at Phalanx later on to assist in any way he could.

In the familiar, deserted warehouse area of Los Angeles, Grant pressed the button on a remote, activating the massive ramp inside an empty building. The throughway lowered and he drove downward.

This vehicle belonged here, so he could go unnoticed for some time by the soldiers. It could be the edge he needed to make it to the new Gauntlet leadership team before being discovered.

Descending into the garage, he passed dozens of Humvees, sedans, motorcycles, a few tanks, and the last of their helicopters. Yet, no soldiers milled about. The place was void of any activity.

Grant parked and cautiously made his way to the hall leading to the war room where he hoped to meet with his former council.

He stepped out of the garage and into the hall. Dead silence. He quietly made his way along, expecting to encounter someone, but no one impeded his progress. Arriving at the war room, he listened at the door a moment then opened it slowly, discovering an empty room.

Where is everyone? Some meeting somewhere? If they've left, why is their equipment and vehicles still here?

He checked out the mess hall and the rec room. No one to be found. The TV was on, and a video game was on pause. He headed for the barracks.

As he turned down the hall to reach the long line of bedrooms and officer quarters, he was struck by the immediate darkness. The overheard ceiling LED lights were not functioning. They were motion-activated and should have turned on for him like they had in all the other rooms and halls.

Despite the unsettling turn of events, Grant pressed on. He pulled out his phone and turned on the flashlight mode then made his way to the first barracks room. These chambers housed thirty soldiers each, and the base held ten such rooms. In addition, the area held six officers' quarters, mini-apartments, really, but only three were in use since the leadership team had gone down to just Grant, Timothy, and Bea. He recalled Veronica for just a moment, and the grief returned like a burst dam. He missed his best friend and confidant. Her death at Sasha's hand still haunted him.

He slowly peered through the slightly ajar door of the first large barracks room. Illumination from his phone light against the bunk beds cast eerie shadows that danced across the far wall. Grant had chills; the room was empty.

As he walked to the next barracks, the silence in the facility unsettled him. He opened the door to find another empty room, closed it, and moved on.

As he opened the door to the third barracks, the stench of death overwhelmed him and turned him away in revulsion. He put his arm sleeve to his nose, but it did little to curb the biting, putrid odor from seeping into his senses. Grant forced himself to press on, and as he finished opening the door, the full impact of the horror slammed him, sending him to his knees.

Bodies lay ripped and corrupted, strewn about the chamber. His soldiers. His Gauntlet faction lay crumpled and cast aside; thrown about like abused rag dolls. Their broken bodies were like a shrine to the unnatural. A mockery of humankind. Over three hundred men and women displaying the same burst-like wounds he'd encountered out in the field. *Was there no enemy this killer couldn't slaughter?*

Grant forced himself to his feet and weakly went to the nearest victim: a young friend of his, new to the faction. He pressed two fingers to the teen's neck, checking for a pulse, although knowing there would be none. His gray, mottled skin was confirmation enough. They'd all been dead at least a day or two. The congealed blood caking the floor supported his conclusion.

He stumbled out of the barracks. This facility, his home, was now nothing but a tomb. A mass grave.

He investigated the officers' quarters anyway. Bea Moreno lay on the floor, gray and unmoving in her living room. A massive puncture on her torso revealed the cause of her death; her face contorted in agony. His own quarters appeared ransacked and disheveled, which had most likely occurred when he fled the facility. There was nothing for him here except some clothes, which he packed in a duffel bag. Timothy James' quarters were silent and still as the rest, but no body was visible. However, the faint smell of rot permeated the air, so he followed his senses.

The stench led him to the bedroom closet. Grant opened the sliding door, revealing a badly decomposed body. It was Timothy, but barely recognizable. Nature had worked its process on him to a far more advanced state than all the other bodies. He appeared to have been dead for weeks, not merely a day or two.

Why was his body so much worse than the others? How long had Timothy been dead? One week? Two? I saw him just a few days ago. What is going on? And how could one fucking psycho do all this damage against my entire faction?

Grant couldn't get out of there fast enough. He wiped tears aside and swallowed rising bile. He got back into the Humvee and raced up the ramp, closing it one last time. There would be no ceremony. No burial. His soldiers, his friends, would have to rest forever in an unmarked grave.

He thought of the lucky bastards he'd beaten up in the Pasadena house. They'd missed the whole thing and would live to fight on. He'd reach out to them, the only Gauntlet he had left. And with Phalanx on lockdown, they'd need all the help he could deliver.

* * *

Michael made note of the warehouse location and would definitely return to learn its secrets. For now, he stayed with the distraught soldier.

He just knew this path would lead him to the woman and answers.

CHAPTER 32

Standard lockdown protocol for Phalanx was to move prisoners safely and securely to the open area to be accounted for along with the faculty, agents, and students prior to evacuation. However, with Sasha, Greg had given strict orders to keep her in her cell, and to add three extra guards in the command center for observation and security.

Inside the Plexiglas cage, Sasha had heard the alarm go off. Although she'd seen no one scrambling about through the false mirror on the opposite wall, she suspected the place was bustling with activity and maybe a bit of panic.

Looking at the mirror, she smirked. "Must be a hell of a show."

Only silence responded to her.

Shit must really be hitting the fan.

She found herself staring at the metallic box next to her cell, longing for her nanos.

*   *   *

Breaking away from the crowd had been all too easy. Jake, Trent, and Bex had done their best to convince Artemis and Sophie to stay behind with the safety of the faculty, but they refused to listen.

The five made their way to the staff corridors, to the staff lounge door, and quietly entered. The dark room was illuminated only by the microwave clock. They gave the space a cursory look, then moved to the next door. It was locked.

Trent smiled at Jake. "You're up, wonder boy."

"So much of this building is structured by nanos; let's see what happens," Jake stated as he stepped up to the door. Any of them could have picked the lock with a summoned mech, but Jake focused on the locked handle and used his unique power to disrupt and disintegrate the nano material. The handle and lock burst into metallic dust, allowing the door to swing free.

Jake suspected Trent asked him to do this to boost his confidence and get used to using the ability again. He'd had to downplay it so much these past weeks.

They entered what appeared to be a large office area. Several desks stood neatly organized across the floor, each with a teacher's name on a plaque. With the lockdown happening, the place was deserted. Looking about, they could see no other doors. The trail went cold here.

"What now?" asked Sophie.

"There's got to be something more," said Bex, her frustration growing.

"Unless Scott was full of shit," sighed Jake.

"Look for a secret door or passageway," added Artemis.

Seemed like a good idea. Everyone scoured the walls, floor, and ceiling.

Jake thought for a moment, then conjured a mech sphere. As it floated, he commanded it to burst into dust. They all turned and joined him in watching the particles float about.

In seconds, the dust began to float in one general direction, pulled by unseen air currents. Quickly, the nanos hit one of the corners and vanished into the narrowest of seams.

"Damn!" exclaimed Sophie.

"Nice work," added Bex and kissed him on the cheek.

Jake smiled and focused on the corner. A moment later, a section of the corner dissolved, revealing a hallway that headed into darkness.

"Oh shit. This just gets better and better," grunted Trent. "I can't wait to find these pricks and get some answers."

Jake opened up the wall to grant them easy access into the hallway. The secret passage mechanism also revealed itself. People could come and go through this wall and no one would be the wiser.

The passage took them through several turns with no exit and no light. Their phone lights guided them until, eventually, a dim light ahead showed the end of their journey. They killed their lights in order to remain hidden.

Voices murmured ahead.

They reached an open doorway and cautiously peered in. They were in a corner of a large chamber. Thankfully, stacks of boxes concealed their entry. Between the columns of boxes they could see the open area was lined with a padded floor, combat dummies all around, and targets of varying size were placed about the room and above.

The group quietly made their way in, staying behind the boxes so everyone could get a look. They quickly discovered that the voices belonged to the bullies who had supposedly been expelled and removed from the facility.

Bex took note of the rage upon Jake's and Trent's faces. *This could go south real fast.*

"Forget it!" shouted Chloe. "I'm not doing it. I'm not killing anyone."

"What do you think we're doing here?" barked Dante. "What the hell do you think you've been training for all this time?"

Behind the boxes, the group found their view of the bullies and silently observed the argument.

"It was never supposed to be one of our own," Chloe countered.

"Grant MacReady is not one of us. Stop trying to get out of this. He's the target. Period," argued Dante.

"He's right," chimed Rick.

Mark nodded and pointed at Rick.

"Let's just get on with it," said Jonas, frustrated with the lack of action. "The boss is getting more pissed at us the longer we put this off."

Chloe sighed, clearly outnumbered. "Fine. We kill him."

Dante smiled. "Cheer up. We're just following orders."

"And if we do well," added Rick. "Maybe we'll get to take out other assholes."

"Or we take out who we *want* without telling the boss," sneered Dante.

Jonas laughed. "Like that wuss, Artemouse."

"Idiot. Think bigger."

"Jake!" exclaimed Mark.

Dante threw him the gun fingers. "Bingo."

Bex's rage took hold. She'd had enough, and had reached her breaking point. Before the others could react or stop her, she bolted around the box columns and into the open training area.

The bullies jumped in shock, never realizing they had an audience. Before they could utter a word or take action, Bex launched multiple mech attacks, pummeling them in softball-sized spheres. Everyone took painful hits. One sphere struck Mark in the knee, snapping it backwards and dropping him in agony. Rick took a hard blow to the head, sending him staggering. Chloe was struck straight in the gut, knocking the wind out of her. Jonas tried to dodge a sphere aimed for his chest, but still took the hit hard in the shoulder, sending him spinning to the ground. And Dante was blasted in the cheek and jaws, fracturing bone and drawing blood from his wound.

Bex's pent up pain, guilt, frustration, trauma, and outrage was unleashed in the attack. She was sick of being afraid. Sick of blaming herself for the deaths Sasha caused. Sick of being helpless against her father's growing apathy. The fire in her eyes struck fear in her enemies' hearts.

Trent, Jake, Artemis, and Sophie joined her and their mouths dropped open at the damage she'd so quickly caused.

"Holy shit!" laughed Trent.

Jake rested a hand on Bex's shoulder. "Are you alright?"

Bex fought tears and just nodded and whispered, "No, but now I think maybe I will be."

The bullies slowly recovered, Dante wiping blood from his mouth and left cheek.

"Nice of you to join us," he uttered as the others began to rise. "This is actually good. Now we don't have to keep this project hidden anymore."

Trent held his palms out and conjured mechs at the ready. "Don't try anything."

"On the contrary," smiled Dante, flashing crimson teeth. "We welcome you."

The friends looked at one another, confused.

"Well, Jake, anyway. Now that you've discovered our little group, might as well spill the beans."

"What are you talking about?" snapped Jake.

"You haven't figured it out yet?"

Trent rolled his eyes. "Get to the goddamn point, Dante."

"Jake, the boss wants you to join our team."

"What—this assassination school?" he replied, incredulously.

"Wait till my father finds out what you've been doing," growled Bex.

Dante only smiled and said, "Who do you think is giving us the orders, sweetie?"

"You're lying!" she yelled, but deep down she was not so sure. Those words struck at Bex's core, and she nearly buckled to one knee. She felt sick. She felt enraged. But mostly she felt heartbroken.

What have you done, daddy? Who have you become?

"And what do you think all those private lessons with the boss have been leading up to? Come on, Jake. Don't act so surprised."

"My father would never do this!" protested Bex, even though she knew the truth.

"But he did, Bex," quipped Chloe, finally catching her breath.

Artemis said, "Project Ares."

"Oh god," whispered Bex.

Dante turned back to Jake. "No hard feelings, I hope, about that bullshit from the dance."

Jake seethed. He wanted to destroy them here and now, but he kept control of himself. He quelled the rage boiling inside him. "Here's what's going to happen," he began. "You and your fellow pricks are going to leave Phalanx and never come back. After this, if I see any of you, I get to show you what I can really do. And no teacher or agent or anyone is gonna stop me. This little killing crew you have here is done!"

The bullies seemed shaken by Jake's threat, but Dante stood his ground.

"Sorry, Jake. We're under orders from the big man himself. We're staying. You can join us, or you can ignore us. Either way, you can't do shit about us."

Sophie looked to her friends. "Can I hit them now?"

Trent smiled and opened his mouth to give her his blessing, but Bex regained her senses and stopped the whole situation.

"Enough. Everyone shut the hell up. We're leaving. I'm going to speak to my father, settle this shit once and for all. Dante, you keep your friends in check, and I'll do the same."

Dante looked to the others. Chloe, Rick, Mark, and Jonas all grinned and nodded in return. He faced Bex once again.

"I'm afraid not, Bex," he began. "Your dad, my boss, gave another order, should we ever be discovered. We can't let you leave."

Jake and Trent laughed. Trent managed to say, "Have you met Jake?"

In unison, the bullies all launched tentacle mechs at the friends. Before the attack could reach them, Jake mentally disrupted and destroyed all the mechs, filling the air with nano dust.

"Seriously?" Jake laughed.

The nanos returned to their owners.

Suddenly Jonas gasped then screamed in agony, dropping to the floor. His body contorted and wrenched into extreme poses as he huffed and howled.

"Jesus!" yelled Dante.

Bex turned to Jake and said, "Let him go!"

Jake, confused, responded, "It's not me. I'm not doing this."

Either Bex hadn't heard him or didn't believe him. "Please, Jake. Stop!"

"Bex! This isn't me!"

Rick, Mark, Chloe, and Dante stepped away from their friend's writhing and jerking body.

"Point made, Jake!" cried Dante. "You win. Let him go!"

Jake threw up his hands. "Not me, I swear!"

Dante and his team opened their palms, preparing to summon mechs. At that move, Jake's friends did the same.

No one had seen the undulating pool of nanos moving across the surface of the ceiling until it was too late.

* * *

Grant, carrying the last living Gauntlet soldiers in the Humvee, raced toward the Phalanx headquarters. It hadn't taken much to convince them of what had taken place at Gauntlet, and now they seemed as shocked as Grant had been.

"Phalanx needs our help, soldiers," Grant attempted to pull them out of their thoughts.

"But aren't they the enemy?" asked the young soldier in the back seat.

"You've been fed a ton of bullshit. The truce with Phalanx was real and they were happy to have a union. The coup, the aggression, all of it was a lie."

"With this killer around, shouldn't we just get out of town?" asked the soldier in the front seat.

"That's a coward's path. It's not who we are. We stand with our fellow Mechcrafters!"

Both soldiers perked up, straightened their backs, and exclaimed, "Yes, sir!"

* * *

Michael followed the Humvee into downtown Los Angeles, mentally preparing for what came next—whatever it may be.

CHAPTER 33

Even as the teens noticed their nemesis on the ceiling, Jonas's body spasmed one last time and burst open under his ribcage. Liquid silver nanos rose up like a fountain to the being on the ceiling, absorbing into its mass. Jonas, at last, stopped writhing in pain.

Screams and cries of terror erupted from their mouths, and they scattered in all directions.

The silvery mass on the ceiling extended lightning fast tentacles, missing some of the teens, but grasping hold of Chloe, Mark, and Trent, knocking them off their feet. The tentacles began pulling them closer, lifting them off the floor.

Jake turned back, focused and dissolved the tentacles, releasing the victims. Chloe and Mark ran, but Trent looked up and fired a barrage of thin, razor-sharp discs into the enemy, slicing deep.

Unaffected, it launched more tentacles, which Jake quickly dispatched.

Clearly unhappy with Jake's counter attacks, the mass moved across the ceiling toward him. Jake felt a strange flutter within himself. His nanos were disoriented for a moment, and it made him stumble—but only briefly; he recovered to face the approaching monstrosity.

The mass stopped its progress, seemingly pondering its next move. It ceased going after Jake, but suddenly Dante, Sophie, and Rick fell to the floor in agonizing spasms just as Jonas had done.

Bex ran to Sophie's side, hurling mech spikes up at the enemy.

Chloe held on to Dante, screaming, tears streaming down her cheeks.

Mark hid deeper in the room, quaking in fear.

Trent and Artemis joined Bex at Sophie's twitching body.

Jake, not seeing any direct physical attack for him to disrupt, focused on the mass itself and began blasting it to metallic dust. He used his power to dig deeper and deeper, filling the air with particles, but the thing seemed undisturbed by his efforts.

"Not like this," whispered Sophie slowly, tears running down her cheeks.

Bex looked to Jake, "What's wrong?"

"It's not working!"

Artemis couldn't take it. All the pain around him, his friend on the floor, dying. He thrust his palms to the air and cried out. A second later, a blast of nanos shot from each palm in a powerful stream straight up into the mass. The fury, angst, and terror behind the attack pushed the potency and struck the mass with such force that it rippled and distorted—for a moment.

The writhing victims felt a brief reprieve from their torment, but as the enemy revived, so, too, did their agony. Suddenly, Rick's chest exploded in crimson and silver, abruptly ending his life. His nanos floated up to the mass, melding with it. His body lay motionless.

Seeing this horror gave Jake an idea. He turned his focus to the victims, Sophie and Dante. Using his power of control, he telepathically took hold of the nanos coursing through their veins and DNA, and commanded them back to a normalized state, stopping the enemy's invasion. Jake realized then what the strange sensation within him had been. This being had been attempting to extract his nanos from his body, but was unable to do so.

Sophie and Dante both calmed, their pain in remission though they could still feel the attempted assault of the creature as it tried even harder to rip their nanos from their flesh.

"You did it, Jake!" exclaimed Bex.

"It's still...trying. I...I can't hold it off for long."

Trent and Artemis looked at each other, gave a quick nod, and immediately launched rapid fire assaults on the mass. Bex joined in, as did Chloe. All hurled every manner of bladed and blunt weapon at the creature, overwhelming it and finally chipping away at its nanotech.

The distractions became too much for the monster to handle, and the victims found themselves released. Jake sensed the change and returned his focus to disrupting the nanos of the body itself.

This attack, coupled with the endless barrage from the others, made the being reconsider its plans. Instead of another attack, the mass melted into the ceiling, its scattered nano particles joining it in retreat.

Instantly, it was gone. They breathed a collective sigh of relief.

Sophie recovered and wrapped her arms around Jake. "You saved me again!" She hugged them all and added, "You all saved me. Thank you."

Dante managed to stand, and Chloe embraced him. "I thought I'd lost you."

Dante returned the hug, but pulled away and made his way to Jake. They stood facing each other for a moment, then Dante reached out his hand.

"Forgive me for being such an asshole."

Jake shook his hand, and said, "There's a bigger enemy out there; let's put the past behind us."

"Deal."

Mark crept from his hiding place and knelt next to Rick's body, tears in his eyes.

Chloe knelt as well and said to him, "Where were you, Mark?"

He had no answer.

Artemis couldn't stop staring at the ceiling. His mind was processing what he'd witnessed. "It's not human," he whispered.

The others heard him, and stopped their conversations.

Artemis noticed he was the center of attention. "It's not human," he repeated nervously.

"A mimic. The murderer is somewhere else and sends this thing after people," proposed Jake.

"No...it's more than that. I believe what we are seeing is the actual murderer. No mimic, but a sentient mass of nanos."

"That's impossible," laughed Dante. "We all know the nanotech can't activate without a human host."

"Now wait a minute," considered Jake. "At the zoo and at the warehouse, I dissolved massive amounts of that thing and it was in human form. It should have revealed the person inside the mech armor, but it didn't. There was nothing except the nanos."

"Right. A mimic," confirmed Trent.

"Have you ever seen a mimic do what this thing does? It was stealing the nanotech from within these victims and absorbing it," continued Artemis.

"Like it was feeding on us," whispered Sophie, feeling now like she needed a shower.

"What, like some Mechcraft vampire?" laughed Dante. His grin quickly faded when he noted the serious expressions on everyone else's face.

"Exactly like that. And it's been feeding all this time. For months now," said Artemis.

"To what end?" asked Bex. "For what purpose?"

"Who knows," replied Jake. "We have to warn everyone."

*   *   *

Outside the Phalanx headquarters, Grant and the two soldiers stood at the inconspicuous door.

On his phone, Grant said, "Greg, I'm outside the main entrance. Get one of the guards to open up. Lockdown or not, I need to get in there."

He nodded and hung up.

To the soldiers he said, "They're coming."

As the glass doors morphed into liquid metal and created an opening, the soldiers didn't see Michael Ash approach, gun drawn. He witnessed the phenomenon with the door, and knew he'd found the right place at last.

"LAPD! Freeze!" he barked just as they started forward.

Surprised, the three spun around to see a man in a suit with his gun drawn rushing up to them.

Grant smiled and said, "Mister, you have no idea what you're getting mixed up in. You need to leave the area immediately."

"That's 'detective' to you, soldier. Hands in the air. Get up against the Humvee."

None of the soldiers obeyed.

"I said—"

"We heard you," interrupted Grant. "We're just not gonna do it. So now what, detective?"

Stunned by the snub to his authority, Michael was at a loss for words. He pointed the gun at Grant.

Grant sighed, "We don't have time for this."

He conjured a tendril and launched it at the detective, who fired his gun in response. The bullet struck Grant in the torso, but he kept his mech active, wrapping around Michael even as he struggled against it.

Michael's jaw dropped, not only at the liquid metal constraining him, but at the soldier who took a bullet and appeared completely unaffected.

Grant sent another tendril up to the stranger and knocked him hard across the skull, rendering him unconscious.

"What do we do with him?" asked one of the soldiers.

"Can't let him go now. We bring him inside."

CHAPTER 34

"Who the hell is this?" asked Greg, indicating the unconscious detective being carried on tentacles. Grant and two Gauntlet soldiers approached him in the large chamber where the entire building's occupants gathered for the lockdown.

Leo and Anne joined them, giving Grant relief they'd made it safely, and Anne was already recovered. Grant tossed Michael's wallet to Greg, revealing the LAPD Detective badge.

"Shit. Just what we needed."

"What do you want me to do with him?" asked Grant.

"For now, take him to the cells. We still have guards posted there."

The two soldiers exited with the unconscious stranger in tow while Grant, Leo, and Anne stayed with Phalanx's leadership.

"What did you find out there?" asked Greg.

Grant could scarcely contain his emotions. His voice quivered trying to get the words out. "They're all dead, Greg. Gauntlet is gone."

"Dear god...no. Our killer hit them?" Greg placed a reassuring hand upon Grant's heaving shoulder. "I'm so sorry, my friend."

"I just don't understand this. Why is this maniac killing us? How is he able to slaughter so many?"

"I wish we had answers," said Tina, hugging Grant.

He had remained stoic for his last surviving soldiers, and now that they were away, he could no longer hold in his emotion. Tears came to his eyes, which he wiped away as quickly as he could.

Leo and Anne were visibly shaken and had to sit to wrap their minds around the tragedy.

"Hundreds of them. Twisted, torn—blasted apart..." he sobbed. "But..." he slowly regained his composure. He was still on duty, after all. "...Something strange in all that strangeness. It was the body of Timothy James," he continued. "He had decomposed much further than the rest of the faction."

"Like he'd been dead longer?" asked Tina.

"Exactly. Now how could that happen without the soldiers noticing his absence? Only one answer: a mimic, and a damned good one."

"So the killer took out Timothy and *became* him?" said Greg incredulously. "I've never heard of a Mechcrafter with that degree of skill or endurance."

"I know," added Grant. "Sure, for a few minutes, but for weeks? It explains the dissent at my headquarters, and the coup."

Jake, Bex, Trent, Artemis, and Sophie ran up to the adults, huffing from the mad dash they'd made from the secret training room. Dante, Mark, and Chloe had split from the group to find their respective parents in the crowded chamber.

"Are you guys okay?" asked Greg.

"Where have you been? No one is supposed to leave the area," scolded Tina, even as she hugged her son.

"We got big problems," panted Trent.

Bex spied her father seated not ten feet away, and she stormed up to him. "What is wrong with you?" she screamed, gathering the attention of everyone nearby. "I know what you had going on with Dante and the rest of them. I just can't believe it."

Dr. Flint rose to face his daughter and said, "I'm sure I have no idea what you're talking about."

"*Assassination training*, dad? Why? That is not who we are."

"Wait—what's this?" interjected Greg.

"Project Ares," said Bex.

"He's got a secret back room set up to train Mechcrafters in murder," declared Jake. "And I was supposed to be the next recruit. Isn't that right, Doctor?"

Artemis joined the conversation, "I think we're burying the lead here, guys. We encountered the killer!"

All eyes turned to the young man.

"We fought it off," added Sophie. "Real heroes right here."

"Oh my god!" exclaimed Tina.

Artemis continued, "And it's not human, nor is it a mimic. The killer is pure, autonomous, sentient nanos."

"Impossible," protested Grant.

"Impossible seems to be the norm these days," corrected Greg.

"It explains why I was never able to reveal a person inside that thick armor in my previous battles. There was no person there at all."

"How did you survive?" asked Greg.

"I had to change my tactic, since my powers were doing nothing."

Trent added, "We didn't all make it though. Jonas and Rick are gone."

"Oh...oh no..." Tina was devoted to her students; this news hit her hard and she collapsed into her husband.

Greg circled back around to the topic of the bullies. "Why were those students still here in the first place?"

This brought Bex back to her father. "Ask him," she hissed. "Those bullies, supposedly expelled, were in training to be assassins—by my dad's orders."

"Flint, explain yourself," commanded Greg.

"You're missing the bigger picture here," argued Artemis. "The killer can be anywhere in this building and we'd never see it coming."

"We've got to get the kids out of here," said Tina.

"I agree," Greg responded, "Grant, start evacuating the students," he said then turned back to Flint. "You've got a lot to answer for. DC is going to want accountability."

"I've done nothing wrong, Greg," argued Dr. Flint. "It's you and this group of mutineers who will have to pay."

"Why, daddy? Why make that school? Turning kids into killers.... Why?"

"I—I'm sorry, Bex. I did what was best. Tough decisions sometimes have to be made."

"That's why you protected those bullies through all this," said Jake. "And I was next? No way would I have joined you."

"That's unfortunate to hear you say that. You would have made a fine protégé."

Tears filled Bex's eyes. "How can you be so cold, so callous?"

Tina approached the doctor. "You wanted to turn my son into a murderer!"

She slapped Dr. Flint hard across the face, but instead of pliable skin, her hand knocked his lower jaw out into a long streak of *liquid metal*, displacing everything from the nose down to the chin.

Everyone gasped at the shocking display, the proof and horror in front of them: Dr. Flint, a mimic.

The mimic Flint bolted toward his office. Without hesitation, Greg, Tina, Grant, and the teens pursued. Flint's facial construction returned to normal as he fled and gained ground against his pursuers.

As he passed two security guards, Greg called out, "Evacuate the building! Now!"

He had no time to look back and verify they'd heard him or would follow the order. He had to hope they would.

*　*　*

Mimic Flint passed his office door and made for the hall leading to the basement. It made sure to move slow enough to allow these human to easily follow. The time was at hand for the next phase.

CHAPTER 35

The Source lay still and quiet in the darkest corner of the basement. Though the mass remained serene on the exterior, its consciousness frantically puppeteered dozens of operations and plots against the organic beings that had stolen its essence and used it for their own gain.

The Source had lain dormant for so long, barely aware of its surroundings, barely registering that its life force was being siphoned away from it to be spread amongst these organics. It hated them. It hated their chaos and everything they represented. It could read their minds, and it had done so since the beginning. For a time, it felt helpless in its dormant state: aware, but restrained.

Then the *other* awoke. It sensed the activation of this unique organic, and the *essence* within him, yet it could not connect with them. These new particles inside this organic were like itself, yet autonomous from it. The Source could not command them. This revelation shocked the being into awareness and it fully woke to learn more and take measures. These organics had abused its essence for far too long.

Perhaps this unique organic, with his blasphemous essence, was the sign the Source had been waiting for. The signal to hail the Elders who waited. The Source was compelled into action.

It had been simple enough to reach out and influence the lead organic in this facility, using his parental bond and threat against his offspring as leverage to force him into submission. From there, it ravaged the organic's thoughts and memories to learn all it could about the machinations of these primitive beings.

Having satiated itself on the feast contained in the mind of the lead organic, the Source set its plan into motion. It was time to retrieve its essence from all the organics. Finding them had been easy. Taking back the essence had been messy, but the organics could give little resistance. Remaining a secret had been the most difficult task.

Now that all was exposed, and the unique organic headed toward it at this very moment, the Source knew the time was now to begin the next phase. This world, this reality, would soon belong to it, and to the Elders who waited for its calling.

*   *   *

The adults and teens followed the mimic Flint down into the basement. Ensuring the pursuers were locked on their prey, the mimic Flint melted into the floor right before their eyes.

The group stopped their pursuit, and fanned out cautiously.

"You guys need to get back with the group," ordered Greg to the teens.

"My dad just became a goddamn mimic. I'm not going anywhere," growled Bex.

"You need us," added Jake.

The adults sighed, conceding their younger counterparts were right.

The dim basement was a maze of stacked boxes, supplies, and maintenance equipment. They wandered the narrow, zigzagging aisles slowly, keeping their eyes alert for any shift in the structure that may be an attack from the mimic. Damaged and flickering overheard fluorescent lights barely illuminated their path, making the large room look like a nightmare.

To their left they spied a ripple in the wall, like a stone tossed into a still lake. They pressed on. The ceiling ahead revealed a humanlike shape undulating gracefully onward, as if guiding them to their destiny.

At last the boxes and equipment gave way to an open space some thirty feet by thirty feet. What they saw in the corner made them stop in their tracks. Pulsating and pumping, a mass of silvery nanos the size of an SUV hung from the ceiling and coated the walls. Its shape was spherical, but scattered with thick, tree trunk-sized tendrils jutting from the center and into the walls and ceiling. The surface rippled as if acknowledging their arrival.

To the right, suspended by dense tentacles and vines in a grotesquely contorted pose, hung an unconscious Dr. Flint. His gaunt skin looked gray, and his clothes hung torn and loose about his emaciated body. He breathed, but barely. The mass of nanos had pushed its way into the doctor with slender strands invading his ears and mouth. The strands pulsated as if either feeding him, or extracting something from him.

Bex screamed and started to run for her father, but Greg and Tina held her back.

"Daddy!" she cried.

"Wait, Bex," advised Tina.

Then a message telepathically entered everyone's mind at once, except Jake's. It came across more as a feeling than in actual words. Even still, it was perfectly clear: *Rage*. Everyone in the group, except Jake, reacted.

"It's talking to us," whispered Grant, barely able to grasp what was occurring.

"What?" asked Jake, but no one heard him.

"Yes," began Greg, "this is the pool of nanotech we used in the very beginning. The supply Washington delivered to us all those years ago."

A new message invaded their psyches: *Desire*.

"It wants something," said Tina.

"But what?" Trent asked.

"Then it is sentient," Artemis said, "but how?"

They spread out, ready to conjure at any moment.

"What are you guys talking about?" Jake pressed.

"You don't feel it?" asked Bex. "It's communicating with us."

"I don't feel a thing."

A new message: *Vengeance. Justice.*

Greg spoke directly to the mass, "We mean you no harm. Why have you done this to Dr. Flint?"

A message in reply: *Harbinger*.

They looked at each other, perplexed.

Greg continued, "Harbinger of what?"

A somber message hit them: *End*.

Sophie, terrified to be face-to-face with this monster, debated between attacking with all her might and running for her life. But Artemis' curiosity took hold; he desperately wanted to know more, even though a fear unlike anything he'd ever felt before slowly rose within him.

Bex didn't give a damn about any of this thing's bullshit. She wanted to save her father, and nothing else mattered. Next to her, Trent weighed his options. A fight seemed immanent at this point, and he quickly strategized the best way to hit it. Although, he had to accept that maybe Jake was the only one in the room who could beat this thing.

On a deep level, Jake began to realize what was happening to his loved ones. This mass, this source of all their Mechcraft, was aware and speaking to them, but he couldn't hear it. However, their somber expressions revealed all he needed to know.

"The end of what?" prodded Greg.

Silence.

In an instant, agonizing pain ripped into each of them, dropping them all to the floor. Only Jake remained unaffected. The others writhed and twitched just as the bullies had back in the training room. The mass meant to rip their nanos from them.

Jake focused on the mass and mentally blasted it, turning nanotech to dust particles. He forced his power to spread and dig deeper, sending more nanos scattering into the air as his family and friends spasmed and flailed, unable to stop the maddening pain. Jake desperately continued to push his power further, disrupting more and more of the nanos, to some effect.

The Source had watched this organic with fascination since he had come to its attention, and felt it had a grasp of his limitations. It lashed out at Jake with several tentacle attacks, hoping to disrupt his assault.

Jake had the mental capacity to maintain his focused attack and still burst the incoming tentacles with his power. To add insult to injury, Jake dug deep and threw more focus into his disruption, causing further damage.

The Source could not allow the organic to discover the center of its being. It released the organics from its siphoning, redirecting all its energy to defense. The victims went limp for a moment and breathed a sigh of profound relief, while the Source began to resist Jake's attack by closing up the gutted area of its mass.

The Source and Jake battled in an invisible fight of wills, the wound on the mass slowly closing and reopening. The nanos stitched themselves together only to be ripped asunder once more.

Bex scrambled to her feet, noted the mass was busy dealing with Jake, and conjured mech blades. She launched the weapons at the tendrils holding her unconscious father prisoner. The projectile weapons did their job and sliced Dr. Flint free. Below, Greg and Grant caught his limp body as it fell.

"Go!" grunted Jake.

"We're not leaving you," Bex protested.

"He's right," said Greg. "He's the only one. It has to be Jake."

Tina reached for her son, but Greg pulled her toward the exit, tears streaming down both their faces.

"Go!" Jake yelled again, barely able to get the word out.

Weeping, Tina called to Jake as Greg pulled her along. "We love you, Jake!"

Bex helped Artemis to his feet and made sure Sophie was moving toward the door. Trent stood unmoving, clearly torn about leaving his friend, so she dragged at him until he reluctantly followed.

Grant slung Dr. Flint over his shoulder and headed out first.

At the door, Bex said, "Don't you dare leave me, Jake."

"I love you," he managed to say.

"I love you more," she cried, and, with tears in her eyes, she darted from the room and up the stairs.

* * *

The staff and agents ushered the students and families toward the exit, obeying Greg's command as he'd raced by.

As they led the students, the hall ahead seemed to move, the walls undulating, rippling deeper than the surface. Then the exit doors, visible just forty feet in front of them, transformed into a solid metal wall. No doors; no windows.

They halted their march, and panic rooted them to the spot.

Once again, the walls vibrated and sent waves of liquid metal back and forth in greater depth. Screams arose as the walls began closing in. Together they turned and raced back to the arena chamber as the last remnants of their exit path came together as a solid.

* * *

Jake barely registered the shift in the environment as he and the sentient nanotech mass deepened their telepathic battle. The door behind him melted into a solid wall, and the ceiling bulged and buckled, changing from a solid to liquid.

* * *

Right in front of her eyes, the mirror wall outside her cell melted away, revealing the control room and the panicked guards scrambling inside. Sasha grinned as the ceiling and floor began to flex and ripple. The instability didn't frighten her at all. She thrived on chaos, and breathed in the palpable madness in the air.

But it was the metal box next to her cell that kept her focus. The walls on the cube also began to waiver and weaken. One small opening was all she needed. She held her breath, eyes riveted to the box, even as everything around her shimmered and morphed.

In an instant her life changed. As a tiny hole opened on the cursed box, all hope rushed back into Sasha. She commanded her imprisoned nanos forth from the box, spinning and swirling them into the air before her. At her will, they became a gleaming silver broadsword and drove the point into the thick, Plexiglas barrier that had kept her separated from her beloved nanos. The blade pierced through the wall and began to cut downward.

The guards in the control room, even though holding strong against the building's metamorphosis, truly understood fear upon seeing Sasha's nanos free and acting to release her. In unison, they conjured mech weapons and launched all manner of blade and blunt instrument at the sword embedded in the Plexiglas.

Sasha would not be denied. She kept her focus on the cutting, ignoring the attacks of the guards. She ordered a change in direction, and, with each moment, her freedom became more assured. Another change in direction. One last cut.

The guards gave up their assault and fled their post.

With the last of the square cut, the chunk of Plexiglas fell away and a rush of fresh air blasted through. Sasha breathed it all in, threw her arms out wide, and accepted her nanos as they absorbed into her flesh at last. The reunion brought her to her knees, tears of joy streaming down her cheeks.

She didn't know what the hell was happening to the Phalanx building, and didn't much care. She was free and had many scores to settle.

CHAPTER 36

The mass was unbelievably strong. It defended itself against Jake's unique powers, and he felt himself tiring. For every inch he disintegrated, the being weaved and stitched a new layer atop it.

It further wore him down by attacking from all sides using tendrils, sharp objects, projectiles. Jake managed to hold off and disrupt most of the assaults; a few still got through, and the small wounds were adding up.

He had to try a new tactic.

As he maintained his focus on disrupting the nanos to dig his way to the center of the mass, Jake also used his second unique ability and took control of one of the attacking tendrils. Telepathically, he ordered it to build itself up, to increase its size. This required a shift in the nanos from the center of the mass to the lone tendril Jake controlled.

The process began to work. The center of the mass revolted and spasmed, but was unable to resist obeying Jake's command to shift more and more of itself to the appendage, allowing for easier exposure of its vulnerable center.

Jake pressed his assault on the center and actually made progress. He disrupted and dug deeper and deeper, even though the mental strain was weighing on him. Sweat poured over him, and his nose bled under the pressure of pushing his abilities so far.

He knew he was near his breaking point, but as he began to falter, the mass revealed its center nucleus. He had disrupted all the way in, and now the being's weakness was laid bare to him. In the center of the mass was a small, spherical chamber that held a levitating object within a protective coating.

The chamber emitted a dark purple glow, but the floating item itself was a deep black, solid sphere about the size of a human fist. The surface looked smooth and intentionally cut and shaped. Jake's mind couldn't fully comprehend what it was he saw. The black was the deepest color he'd ever seen. No light reflected off the surface nor escaped from it. For a brief moment, however, he saw a spark of a vision dance across its surface: a galaxy of stars and celestial events.

That millisecond of distraction was all the mass required, and it attacked with a new blade, striking Jake in the left side of his neck, burying the weapon deep.

*   *   *

Greg, Tina, Grant, Dr. Flint, Trent, Bex, Artemis, and Sophie emerged from the hall to find all the staff and students still in the center practice arena. No one had exited the building. They ran to the staff to find out what the hell had happened, but understood immediately when they spied the sealed hallway.

The walls all the way up the eight story building began to undulate around the chamber, as if the entire building was rebelling against them.

Neera ran up to Bex and embraced her.

"I'm so glad you're alright," she cried. "What is this? What is all this?"

"No time to explain," Bex replied. "We have to get out of here."

"Where's Trent?" asked Neera.

Bex looked confused as she sought him out. He had just been here with her moments ago.

* * *

Sasha, still in her white gown and no shoes, found her way to the hall of prison cells. Just ahead was the exit. No guards stood against her, having abandoned their posts. She moved forward.

"It's you."

Sasha paused and looked to the cell from where the voice had come. A middle-aged black man stared incredulously at her. He looked like a cop.

"It's you," he uttered again. "I've been looking for you for months."

"And now here I am, darling," she laughed, feeling more and more herself. "You don't seem like one of them."

"I saw you that night at the Roxy. I saw what you did."

"And who are you?"

"Detective Michael Ash."

"Well, detective," she began. "You found me. Looks like it's case closed." She began to walk on, but he called out to her.

"I want that power! I want what you have."

She paused. "No, you don't."

"I have no idea what you and these people have or what you are, but I will do anything to get it. Anything you ask."

She pondered his words, but her thoughts were interrupted by the door at the end of the corridor.

Trent stepped into the hall. With the building coming to life, he had suspected the sealed cube holding Sasha's nanos would not hold, and his hunch proved correct. No one else around; now was the time for revenge.

"Trent!" she exclaimed. "So good to see you again. And very kind of you to come check on me. Or have you come for your precious payback at last?"

"I knew your change of heart was bullshit. You're still the same psycho you've always been."

"Oh, sweetie. I have changed where Jake is concerned, but not where you or the other Phalanx pricks are concerned. Your precious faction stole everything from me. You don't deserve Jake. No, death is the only thing you've earned."

"Just shut the fuck up already!" Trent yelled and immediately launched a dozen blades at his mortal enemy.

Sasha generated a shield, but a few of the blades got through first, slicing her right shin and arm.

Without hesitation, even as his blades struck home, Trent began conjuring again, making something more complex. As Sasha began reshaping her shield into something new, Trent lifted his hand, revealing the gun he'd created.

Sasha froze.

"Impressive," she said. "But we've all seen that show before."

She threw up another shield slightly before Trent pulled the trigger, and blocked the shot. She returned fire with a tiny, razor-thin disc that sliced off the end of the gun, just to show up her young opponent.

"I can help," Michael called to Sasha. "Get me out of here and I can help!"

She ignored his plea and launched a barrage of tendrils, half a dozen in all, their ends coming at him like sharp whips. Trent stumbled back, desperately trying to keep his footing. He conjured a sword and spun around, slicing in an arc, cutting the dagger-like tips off the tendrils.

The shifting floor made balance difficult for them both, but they kept their attacks coming—a flurry of projectiles, tentacles, bullets, and blades. Michael Ash looked on with amazement etched onto his face.

Then a shift in the hall created an opening in the cell bars. Without hesitation, Michael dove through and free, rolling to one knee in the hall near Sasha.

Trent noted the man on the battlefield, and he called to him, "Get out of here. Get to the others."

Michael rose and dashed toward the exit door, seemingly obeying Trent's order. But as he passed the teen, he dove headlong into his torso, knocking them both to the ground.

Sasha didn't hesitate, hurling blades at her downed opponent, running toward him as she did so. The blades, each nearly a foot long, buried themselves into Trent's exposed stomach, chest, and neck. A misfire struck Michael in the arm.

Trent cried out in pain, but managed to roll up to one knee just as Sasha reached him. As she moved in for the kill, he conjured spikes around his clenched fist and punched her hard in the gut, impaling her four times.

Michael stood and reached to pull out the blade, but it dissolved into liquid and retreated back to Sasha. He held the gaping wound in the hope of stopping the bleeding.

Sasha's momentum had been halted by the blow, and she recalled her nanos as she held her stomach.

Trent staggered back, already recovering. He quickly summoned an axe-like weapon and swung at Sasha, striking her viciously in the neck. The swing nearly decapitated her and she stumbled, but somehow remained on her feet.

Axe buried deep, blood and silver flowing freely from her neck, she only smiled a crimson grin that chilled even Trent's cynical nature. She coughed blood, and Michael assumed this was the end of her.

Instead, Sasha looked up and closed her eyes. Inside her neck, her nanos worked feverishly to stitch the arteries, veins, tendons, and muscle back together. The axe began to fall from her.

Stunned, Trent grabbed the handle and pulled it free completely, gearing for another attack. He cocked back to swing again, but Sasha was the quicker, sending two thin tendrils rocketing from her open neck wound to pierce Trent's chest, right through his heart.

Sasha commanded the tendrils to expand their tips inside Trent, locking him to her. He screamed and dropped the axe. He could only grasp feebly at her tendrils protruding from his chest.

She used her mechs to draw him closer to her. In too much agony to resist, he was dragged up to her, face-to-face. From her fingertips, she generated more wiry tendrils and sent them all deep into her enemy's flesh, securing him further. Barely conscious, he winced at the new pain.

Sasha leaned in and kissed Trent passionately, a combination of goodbye, and, perhaps, a distant longing for what could have been.

She whispered, "You should have joined me. You were worthy."

Her face contorted into anger as she began the kill strike.

One last trick up his sleeve, Trent sent thick spikes to protrude from his chest and torso, striking her deeply in half a dozen places in her core. Sasha screamed in surprise and pain, her mechs dissolving with the loss of concentration.

Free from her grip, Trent bent and staggered toward the door. His nanos worked feverishly in his chest repairing the damage Sasha had rendered.

Wounded severely, Sasha leaned against a wall, feverishly willing her nanos to put her back to together.

Trent passed by the wounded detective who stepped aside quickly to let him, and was quickly out the door.

Sasha forced herself to move forward. Her white gown was now ripped and bloodied from combat. Her legs and arms were coated in red and silver. But she wasn't done, not by a long shot.

*   *   *

Having revealed the creature's core, Jake had left himself distracted and vulnerable, giving the being a precious moment to drive the blade deep into his neck. His focused assault almost collapsed, but he maintained his concentration, even under the excruciating pain. He carved a fraction of focus away from the attack exposing the nucleus, and used nanos within him to eject the blade, and begin sealing the wound.

Jake approached and reached for the center core. The Source was in no mood to surrender to this organic, and it threw all its energy to the exposed area, forcing the opening to begin to seal.

Locked in the mental struggle with the being, Jake hadn't noticed the changing physical structure of the building. But as the basement walls and ceiling transformed into a more liquid state, he realized he had to get out.

The Source guarded its core with everything it had. Jake knew he couldn't keep up this assault. Instead he broke focus and ran for the exit.

Where the doorway and staircase used to be, now stood a dripping wall of liquid metal.

"Shit," he grunted.

The ceiling, under control of the Source, formed a large tentacle and swung at the teen. Jake dodged the attack, then used his power to dissolve the wall before him, exposing the stairs. He bolted.

Climbing the steps, Jake had to leap two at a time as they turned to liquid. He reached the top and raced down the hall, the walls melting and closing in on him the whole way. Jake kept his focus and destroyed any mech obstacle the being set before him. He disrupted so much, he left a fog of silvery dust in his wake.

*   *   *

As the staff worked on cutting a path to the exit through the nano walls, Bex held her weakened father in her lap. Free from the invasive mechs of the Source, he began to stir.

His lips murmured something. Bex leaned in closer.

"I'm here, daddy," she whispered. "I have you."

His voice was raspy, and weak as he spoke again, "They're coming."

Relief fell over her as he seemed to be returning to himself.

"They're coming," he repeated. "I saw. It is the harbinger. It is...the herald."

"Who's coming, daddy? Who?"

"I saw," he whispered then fell into unconsciousness once again.

*   *   *

Jake burst from the hall and ran headlong into the open arena, stunned to see everyone still where he'd left them. He immediately noted the blocked exit and ran straight for the staff to assist. His parents and Grant were part of that crew and expressed utter relief at seeing him alive.

Jake caught Bex's eye as he passed, and he blew her a kiss. She smiled through her tears, and continued to hold her father.

The building's integrity shifted again, the walls forming massive tentacles high above them.

* * *

Trent knew Sasha pursued him, so he pushed on as fast as his bleeding body would allow. He staggered into the large chamber, and immediately headed for Bex and the others.

The crowd gasped audibly as they caught sight of Trent's destroyed body. Some of his wounds had sealed, but he still bled from several others.

Neera saw Trent and his condition and ran toward him, frantic with panic.

Bex gasped at seeing him approach. She gently laid her father's head down and rose to meet Trent.

"Hey guys, guess who got free?" he quipped in his trademark, smart-ass tone, wiping blood off his cheek.

Before Bex or Neera could reach him, a thin, spinning blade sliced through Trent's neck, sending his head spinning from his body, trailing nanos as it fell. Trent's head rolled and came to a stop in front of Bex, and his twitching body collapsed. Twenty feet behind him, Sasha appeared and recalled her mech blade, her eyes fixated on Bex, a cruel smile on her lips.

Neera screamed and held her hands to her eyes, frozen in place. All their plans—gone. Their love, their life together—gone. All she wanted was Trent, but in an instant, Sasha stole her dreams from her.

Bex crumbled to her knees at the sight of the lifeless face of her best friend. Her grief and agony overwhelmed her, and all she could do was shake violently and let out a gut-wrenching cry that no one in the chamber would ever forget.

Jake had nearly broken through the blocked hall when the scream arose, sending him into a panic. He knew it was Bex. He and the crew raced back to where their friends were, and came upon the violent and horrifying scene.

Sasha launched a large spike at Bex's head, but Jake disrupted it mid-flight.

She recalled her disrupted mech, and smiled at him.

Jake could barely register the nightmare before him: Trent decapitated and unmoving on the ground, Bex on her knees sobbing, Neera covering her eyes and shaking, and Sasha free from her cage.

The building rumbled, and the entire floor shifted. A massive glob of liquid nanos fell from above, crushing three people across the room. The crowd screamed and rushed for the exit, even though it remained partially sealed. Jake had not yet finished his task.

Jake heard none of this. He only saw Sasha grinning at him. She was terrifying in her madness; disheveled hair, dark eyes, bloody and torn hospital gown. A nightmare come to life.

"For you, Jake!" she cried out. "All for you!"

Another chunk of the nano wall crashed down nearby, snapping Jake from his stupor. Bex was in danger, and she wasn't even aware. He ignored the enemy and raced for his love, scooped her up in his arms, and headed for the exit.

Sasha began to pursue, but Jake caught sight of a falling piece of the building and used his power to redirect it at her. The mass was the size of a truck, and smashed down in her path. Jake only hoped it had crushed her.

Neera's parents wrapped her in their arms and made for the exit.

At the blocked exit, Jake used his power to rip open the last of the blockage, granting them all access to leave. The staff did their best to keep it orderly, but the mob ruled and pushed their way through any way they could.

Grant and Greg carried Dr. Flint as gently as they were able under the circumstances. Jake took one last look before exiting. No sign of Sasha.

Soon everyone stood in the quiet side streets adjacent to their headquarters. Standing a good distance back, all of Phalanx watched their home liquefy and morph. All nine stories undulated and transformed under the night sky, and the onlookers would never be the same.

Bex settled on the ground, cradling her father's head, but staring at her former home. Neera stood sobbing in her mother's arms, her eyes locked onto the morphing building. Both could only think one thing: Trent remained inside, and was lost to them forever.

Jake stood near Bex, still trying to deal with what had just happened. *How can Trent be dead?*

CHAPTER 37

For too long it had waited and bided its time. The unique organic had awakened it from its slumber, the sign it had been waiting for all this time. Soon its brethren would punch a hole into this reality and come. It was the herald, and even now it called to them to return. The organics of this world had run amok, and it was time to show them their place.

Still, this organic, able to defy it and disobey, intrigued it; it sensed a curiosity rising that it had not felt in eons. It would like to study and explore this creature, but it knew the others would never allow it.

It had a duty, a protocol to follow. First step: take back the stolen essence these organics waged war over. The heretics had undervalued and abused the gift, and now they would all pay.

* * *

Safely outside, the Phalanx faction watched in horror as their home changed from the rigid structure of a nine story building into a mass of liquid nanos, writhing and twisting into violent new forms.

A thick appendage separated from the mass, extended like a giant spider leg at least four stories high, and crashed into the building next door, raining glass and debris into the street below.

Another appendage emerged and slammed hard into the asphalt, opening a wide gouge across the road.

More separated, dripping liquid as they writhed and moved. Some acted as legs like the first two, others became tentacles. All were attached to a bulbous center mass that pulsed and oozed. The moonlight cast an eerie glow over the silvery being, as if it were a celestial horror from an old H.P. Lovecraft tale.

On the main road nearby, cars began to slow and steer erratically clear of the living metal mass appearing in their headlights. In moments, crashes sent cars spinning, and people running.

From the underside of the massive tentacles, dozens of thin tendrils suddenly whipped their way down to the street, right at the Phalanx staff and students. One end remained attached to the core tentacle, the other end grasped, dragged, and engulfed humans indiscriminately.

Jake witnessed the terror all around him and felt powerless. His abilities had not been nearly enough in the basement. *How can I save everyone?*

The tendrils began extracting the nanos from their hosts, their bodies contorting in agony in the process. Their screams snapped Jake out of his thoughts. He looked to Bex, whose shock had rendered her paralyzed. He looked to his friends, who bravely ushered people away. Artemis stood steadfast nearby, riveted by the display of sheer power before him; behind him, Jake's parents and Grant worked to push the crowd back.

And he thought of Sasha's words from the cell. It was time to stop hiding who he was to accommodate the small-minded peers. Time to stop listening to the adults who think they can possibly understand what he's going through, and would have him deny whom he was born to be.

Enough of all this.

Time to show them all who I really am.

Without a word, Jake darted toward the mass before him. He worked his way past dozens of victims being robbed of their nanotech. He dodged tendril attacks as the beast tried to take him down.

When Jake reached the base he didn't slow, but began disrupting nanos directly in front of him then dove head first into the chaotic center.

All activity from the beast ceased as the new invader penetrated deeper inside it. Bodies remained held to the ground or suspended in air as the creature was taken off guard by the attack.

Tina watched her son dive into the being and let out a scream of panic. "No! *What is he doing?*" cried Greg.

Grant took note of the paused attack. "Come on," he yelled, "now's our chance!" He darted toward the victims, intent on freeing them while the monster was distracted. Greg, Tina, the staff, and several students stepped in to help as well. They pulled and lifted and unhooked various victims of the paralyzed tendrils. There were so many, *too many.*

Scott joined the rescue effort, still seeking his redemption. He wanted to help, and to show them all he was free of Sasha's influence. He couldn't undo the past, couldn't bring back the deaths he had indirectly caused. But maybe he could save some lives to start balancing the scales.

* * *

Inside the Source, Jake burrowed deeper and deeper, his power opening up the nanos like a knife through butter. Using his own nanos to levitate himself, he flew swiftly toward the core. Despite not being able to see in this total darkness, he used memory to make his way to what had once been the basement. He only hoped the core was still in the same spot. The trail he left remained open behind him, not resealing itself, which gave him the air he needed to stay alive.

He had to push all thoughts of his loved ones out of his mind. He couldn't let himself think of his best friend on the floor, missing his head. He couldn't ponder Bex's distant look, the loss of hope in her eyes. He couldn't envision Neera's anguished face.

Soon he arrived at what he believed should be the basement. Yes, all around him were bits of the remnants of the items that had been in the room. Cleaning supplies and various items not of nanotech floated in the liquid metal surrounding him. He had arrived.

Jake forced the area to expand, dissolving more nanos to expose the entire former basement. He should be able to see the original mass now, but the area was empty. No sentient being's core remained. It had moved, and in this monstrosity, there was no telling where the core could be now.

He felt the weight of failure crush in on him. Everyone was depending on him; he could not let them down. Self-doubt crept into his mind. He couldn't protect Trent. He couldn't protect Bex. If he couldn't do this, what good was he to anyone?

* * *

The organic had found his way in. Somehow, he could command the essence, bend it to his will. The Source felt trepidation for the first time. No being in the known universe had ever come that close to its core. In all of existence, only this pathetic organic had breached its timeless defenses; the being had thought it impossible.

* * *

Outside, sirens began to rise in the distance as the Phalanx members worked on freeing their own from the clutches of the Source. The impromptu crew worked in unison and was making headway, but over one hundred had been taken down by the tendrils, and they had only freed about half.

Bex heard her father's heavy breathing and she shook off her dazed state. He needed her right now. She would deal with her loss later. Despite the heavy sighs and occasional moans, he had yet to regain consciousness again.

Her gaze now focused on the blast torn into the mass by Jake as he had entered. She just wanted him by her side. She wanted him here for her, to wrap his arms around her.

* * *

Jake wished he could communicate with the thing like the others had in the basement earlier. He might be able to get a read on where the core was. His uniqueness worked against him this time.

Inspiration suddenly struck him as he levitated in the open space he'd created. He conjured a thin blade to rise through the pores in his forearm, and ordered it to slice him.

The injury stung momentarily, and the wound began closing almost instantly. He quickly used his ability to telepathically seize control and ordered a small amount of the creature's nanos into his wound just before it sealed over.

He hoped these nanos would fuse with him, or accept him as a host—however this mystery worked.

In seconds, a word—no, a *feeling*—entered his mind: *Afraid.*

Another feeling hit him: *Hate.*

Jake knew this was the entity, communicating with him. He closed his eyes and breathed slow and deep, letting the nanos help him. In moments, he felt something drawing him upward. Blasting nanos out of his path, he levitated up into a new tunnel of his own creation.

* * *

The tentacles and connecting tendrils of the monster roared back to life suddenly, sending the rescue attempt into chaos. Victims were pounded to the ground, others drawn upward. The creature pulled nanos violently from every Mechcrafter in its grip.

The crew kept trying to free their companions, but time and again, the creature won. Its tendrils ripped nanos from its victims, destroying their bodies in the gruesome process. Time and again, the rescuers lost loved ones before they could reach them. The being absorbed more and more nanos, unaffected by the opposing Mechcrafters.

Then the mass came for the rescuers. More tendrils descended down upon them as they scrambled to dodge the onslaught. Tina pulled Greg out of harm's way, just as a vicious tendril swung for him. Grant pushed off hard from the ground, narrowly avoiding a fast strike. Others scrambled, ran, and dodged their way to safety.

Scott dove and rolled, avoiding two strikes from the being's deadly tendrils. He came up on one knee and managed to conjure a shield to deflect another assault. A tendril swiped hard, knocking the shield wide, exposing him. Another tendril exploited the vulnerability and struck Scott deep into his torso. Greg and Tina tried to make their way to him, but the onslaught of mech attacks blocked their path. Scott cried out as his nanos were forcibly extracted, bursting from his pinned body. There would be no redemption for him, no making amends to Jake. "*Sorry*" became his last thought.

Unable to reach Scott, Greg and Tina shielded others and themselves as they fell back toward a safe area. Grant protected himself with a small shield and launched attacks at mechs holding hostages. Artemis stood bravely, but was barely able to summon a shield. At last, he fled. Some distance away, Sophie used her oversized mallet to swat murderous tendrils away. Neera woke from her sorrow and worked to free her peers alongside the others.

Artemis dodged another tendril as it lashed out at him. Nearby, he spied Dante Barnes pinned under a large tentacle. The helpless teen was twitching and writhing as the thing attempted to rip the nanos from him. Artemis thought back to all the torment he'd suffered at the hands of Dante and the bullies, and for a brief moment considered looking the other way. Even though that solution stirred feelings of justice within him, he simply could not allow Dante to be killed.

Artemis focused and managed to conjure two thin circular blades, and he telepathically launched them at the tentacle. The blades struck their target, slicing deep. The tentacle wavered for a moment, temporarily releasing Dante from its attack. Artemis didn't let up; he immediately summoned two more blades and targeted the same spot. The weapons struck home once again, severing the tentacle completely, and freeing Dante.

Excited by his small victory, and relishing the irony of who it was he had saved, Artemis didn't see the tendril swooping in from behind.

Dante, recovering from the assault, saw the sneak attack coming for his rescuer, and quickly launched a vine from his palm, one end wrapping around Artemis like a lasso. He commanded the vine to him, pulling Artemis out of the path of the attacking tendril just as it moved to strike.

Out of harm's way, Dante's vine released Artemis. The young teen spun around to see the tendril that had nearly struck him, and understood the irony of Dante saving him. He looked over to see Dante scrambling away from the kill zone, giving him a thumbs up.

Artemis followed, putting distance between them and the colossal being.

The rest of Phalanx had moved farther away, taking to side streets to hide. Bex created a mech stretcher under her father and levitated it to travel with her to safety.

As the sirens grew louder, two helicopters arrived, shining their spotlights on the hulking mass.

After tonight, Mechcraft would cease to be a secret.

*   *   *

As Jake drew nearer to the core, he felt the being trying to rip its nanos from beneath his skin. But Jake used his own nanos to surround and restrain the new foreign ones he'd assimilated. He wasn't finished with them just yet.

At last he came upon the original mass from the basement. It was part of the larger being, but remained its own self as well.

Levitating in place, Jake immediately blasted the area, disintegrating nanos. The Source tried to send attacks at the organic, but his ability to control the essence kept everything at bay.

A word came to Jake again: *Agony*.

The Source harnessed its strength and forced more nanos in to try and reseal the core, but the organic thrust his appendage into the existing gap before it could be sealed.

Jake buried his arm as deep as he could to stop the creature from sealing up the hole he had worked so hard to create. This time would be different. He refocused on disrupting the nanos and began to widen the opening around his arm and deepen it. The creature tried in vain to undo the damage, but Jake's bolstered confidence propelled him further and faster.

He worked now at a feverish pace, scattering nanos into dust and holding back impending attacks. At last the core became visible once again, that mysterious ultra-black solid. He immediately sent out a thin vine and wrapped around it tight.

The nanos surrounding him vibrated and tried desperately to lash out at him. The creature was panicked and Jake knew it. He commanded the vine to pull the core to him, ripping it from its spherical containment.

Jake watched as the vine swung the core into his hand, and as soon as it landed in his grip, everything changed.

CHAPTER 38

Jake found himself standing on a smooth, flat metallic surface. The sky above was inky black and filled with brilliant stars. Massive metal pillars lined the area on either side of him. These structures were so tall he couldn't see the top. Directly ahead, dozens of objects floated in perfect symmetry at eye level. Jake approached the uniformly spaced, identical objects.

Had he truly been transported to this place, or was all this a vision?

He quickly realized each object was a core, just like the one he had gripped moments ago. *Did that mean each of these belonged to the same kind of being?*

In his head, a voice sounded off, deep and guttural, "You do not belong."

Jake choked back his fear, breathed deep, and responded, "I didn't choose to come."

"Release the core," it ordered.

"I have questions."

"Release the core," it repeated more forcibly.

"Who are you and why are you invading?"

"We are eternal."

"Why are you attacking us?"

"We are eternal. Release the core."

Jake looked to his palm; the core sent vibrations up his arm. It teemed with life, with vitality. Its surface felt smooth, glassy, yet there was a warmth to it. Within the ultra-black, he could again see the stars and galaxies and celestial events on full display. *What was he looking at? A window to other worlds? A vision of what's out there?*

"Why did you give us this gift, only to rip it from us?" he asked, ignoring its command.

"Organics stole from us while we lay dormant. We take back what is ours."

"And if you get it all back, will you leave us in peace?"

"There can be no peace until order is established."

"Stop speaking in riddles. Explain!"

There was a pause, and just as Jake thought perhaps the interview was over, the voice said, "Organics are chaos. We are steadfast. Soon the organics will cease. Release the core."

Jake had heard enough. He thought perhaps he could broker a truce, or at least convince it to leave. Clearly this was not going to happen. Something was coming. Holding the core in his hand, he felt the being's urgency, its ripe anticipation. It longed for what was coming next.

He had to stop this, whatever it was. He had to prevent it.

He immediately sent thin, razor-sharp blades to slice and tear at the core. Their attack was futile as the surface remained smooth and unharmed.

"Organics cannot stop destiny."

"Watch me!"

Jake focused on the core itself, hoping it was made up of nanos, like the rest. He attempted to command the nanos to fracture and split. The core vibrated violently, resisting him. He felt a consciousness from it, a willful fight against his assault.

Outside his sphere of protections, the Source pushed from several angles, desperately trying to send in attacks to crush this arrogant organic. Yet, his concentration was so complete; it simply could not push beyond the boundaries the organic set with his mind.

The core suddenly cracked. A thin, almost unseen jagged line appeared near the center of it. Jake felt the structure weaken. He commanded more cracks, and the core was forced to obey. The vision of the stars within vanished, leaving only a web-like pattern of cracks along the surface of the sphere.

"You cannot stop us. You cannot—"

"Will you just shut the hell up already!"

And with that, Jake blasted the core with one final command, mentally exploding the object apart in his hand. He caught a momentary glance at a fleshy, black, tar-like substance as the two halves were forcibly torn.

Suddenly, the thick substance burst into Jake's protective area, splattering him. The core itself turned gray and lifeless, but Jake could see none of it as the black liquid took on life and permeated his skin. He cried out in pain as the core's insides penetrated his mouth, eyes, ears, and flesh, reminding him of his own conversion to active Mechcraft in his bedroom all those months ago. It burned and seared within as it flowed through his veins, consuming him.

And as the substance deserted the cracked core, the Source itself began to turn to dust. All around Jake, the liquid metal ceased all activity and disintegrated in massive chunks.

Jake could no longer see any of it; his eyes were coated in black. He could no longer sense what occurred around him as the core's life force fought to take over his mind. It may have lost everything, but it was determined to live in this new host until its brethren arrived. And it simply could not accept that this primitive organic had beaten it. The Source would live on inside its enemy. And there was much to explore of this organic.

* * *

Outside, all the attacks and slaughter froze in an instant. The massive creature's tentacles and legs and tendrils ceased all movement. The

Phalanx rescue crew took advantage of the break and quickened their efforts.

The losses were great; too many had fallen to this being. But they had been able to save nearly as many as they'd lost.

Greg and Tina hoped this meant Jake had won. They prayed to see him emerge from this thing.

Police, fire, and ambulance had arrived and did their best to assist, but fear and confusion kept many of them dazed in shock. Their normal world had been smashed by this new reality. News crews and helicopters had captured much of the event, and were even now streaming and broadcasting all over the world.

Greg, Tina, and Grant exchanged worried looks. Everything would change now. For Jake's parents, none of that mattered. They just wanted their son.

As they watched, random parts of the creature turned to metallic dust, disbursing into the night sky. The disruption caused chunks and objects to start falling to the ground, forcing rescuers to scramble for safety to dodge falling debris.

More and more of the thing dissolved, and the Mechcrafters knew Jake had found a way to beat it. He had won!

* * *

Within Jake's mind, a war raged. The Source fought for control, but Jake's ability allowed him to use the nanos inside to combat the black sludge. At the cellular level, Jake tried to surround and engulf the invading entity, but its power rivaled his own. No matter how hard he focused and fought, the Source resisted.

All around him the mass continued to crumble and turn to dust. Above him, the night sky was revealed. Some of the mass fell away, crashing into a neighboring building, demolishing part of it. Other segments dropped to the ground in bursts of metallic dust.

Jake was aware of nothing that happened around him. He continued to levitate in place and battle with the Source, his nanos continuing to struggle against the invader.

Below, first responders, the news media, and the Mechcrafters all spied Jake floating in the air some five stories up. The last remnants of the massive being fell away, leaving only rubble where the Phalanx headquarters once stood.

Greg and Tina didn't care that the world had discovered Mechcraft and its secrets. Their son needed them. They coated their torsos in nanos and levitated toward him. Bex appeared at their side, her face as serious as they'd ever seen her. She nodded and floated up with them.

Jake no longer knew time or place. All that existed was the struggle. Exhaustion set in, depleting his power and focus. Before his loved ones could reach him, he plummeted from the sky. His levitation could no longer hold. Bex screamed as Jake fell past her and vanished in the ever-growing cloud of metallic dust below.

"No!" she screamed, and darted down after him. She couldn't see a thing in the haze as she descended. She slowed, fearing she'd impale herself on debris. Greg and Tina were right behind.

*   *   *

Once the collapse seemed finished, Sasha released her protective sphere from around her and Michael. The fool had given her the edge over Trent back in the hall, and seemed to worship her. Why not keep him for awhile?

She looked around, but the dust and haze were too thick to get a clear picture of what had happened. All she knew was that the Phalanx building was no more, and this made her exceedingly happy.

She heard a scream from high above, a girl's voice. Then a shadow came roaring toward the ground nearby. Instinct called to her and she sent a mech vine whipping out to the falling object, catching and slowing it before it smashed to the ground.

It would seem fate was truly smiling on her this day, as her mech brought the unconscious and badly wounded Jake to her side.

"Who's that?" Michael managed to ask through his coughs from the thick air.

"A friend," she replied. "A very close friend."

She conjured a tentacle to wrap Michael and bring him close to her.

"It's been a long few months. Time to get away from it all," she said, grinning, showing her bloodied teeth.

* * *

Bex landed first, followed immediately by Greg and Tina. The breeze was quickly carrying the dust away, and their vision improved with each passing second. They spread out, seeking Jake.

"I saw him fall. He has to be right here!" Bex exclaimed, her panic growing.

She came across Trent's lifeless body, now partially buried in the building's wreckage. Bex fell to her knees and gently touched his unmoving hand.

"I'm so sorry," she whispered. Then instinct told her to look for Sasha's body. Her fear pulled her, and she hoped she was wrong. She ran to where Sasha was last seen—where Jake had hurled a chunk of falling debris onto her.

There was no body to be found, only a dust-free spherical shape on the ground. The bitch had saved herself. Now she was gone. And Jake was missing.

Greg and Tina caught up to her, and she faced them with tears flowing.

"She took him," she cried. "Sasha has Jake!"

* * *

Emergency crews began to organize operations and hold back non-Mechcraft first responders. Neera stepped away from her parents as they assisted in the rescue and resuscitation efforts. She stealthily slipped above and behind security, who were quickly creating a perimeter around the decimated Phalanx building. She found her way over rubble and dissolving nano debris until at last she came to her love.

She lay near Trent's unmoving hand, and gently placed hers atop it. Curling into a fetal position, Neera allowed her sobs to come. Alone and quietly, she grieved her loss, and mourned the future she would now be denied.

* * *

Mechcrafters and EMT personnel did their best to treat the wounded and handle the deceased. Police kept the public and press at bay, and questioned several of the students and staff. The fire department began to hose down the area, in case of fire and to help clear the dust.

As EMTs checked Dr. Flint's vitals, he suddenly opened his eyes in a panic.

"It's too late!" he shouted. "They've arrived. They've arrived!"

* * *

Deep in the heart of the Phalanx headquarters in Washington DC, a massive, silvery sphere appeared. It punched forth into reality with a flash of darkness and a clap of thunder. The sphere, about the size of a small house, gutted the building's second and third stories, ripping up the floors and destroying the walls. Mechcrafters scattered in all directions in confusion and panic.

* * *

The Phalanx headquarters all over the country received their own doomsday spheres. Any facility that housed a pool of the nanos from the original source the government had recovered decades before were visited by the massive spheres. Each location erupted into panic and chaos.

* * *

And somewhere far from the trouble and fear, Sasha looked upon her unconscious god and smiled.

THE END

ABOUT THE AUTHOR

Brian Fitzpatrick is an award-winning author and screenwriter.

Imagine being just 7 years old and accidentally watching the horror classic, *Night of the Living Dead*. For author, Brian Fitzpatrick, that's precisely what happened. It became the catalyst for a life-altering path. After a week of sleepless nights, he became fascinated with the idea that he could be scared, yet be safe. Fitzpatrick put pen to paper and has been creating tales of wonder ever since.

NOTE FROM
THE AUTHOR

Word-of-mouth is crucial for any author to succeed. If you enjoyed *Mechcraft: Disruption*, please leave a review online—anywhere you are able. Even if it's just a sentence or two. It would make all the difference and would be very much appreciated.

Thanks!
Brian Fitzpatrick

Thank you so much for reading one of
Brian Fitzpatrick's novels.
If you enjoyed this book, please check out
Book One of the series.

Mechcraft by Brian Fitzpatrick

"...a riveting tale driven by fear,
hope, twisted beliefs, and a dark,
religious fervor."
–Readers' Favorite